D0046276
014
5
VE NOV 2016
RU JUL 2018

Photograph © Carolyn Haslett

The author of seventeen books, Stacy Gregg has reinvigorated the pony genre with her two popular series *Pony Club Secrets* and *Pony Club Rivals.*

A former journalist, Stacy undertook extensive research, travelling to Jordan with the blessing of Princess Haya. Given unprecedented access to the palaces and royal stables, she conducted lengthy interviews with Her Royal Highness, Her family and friends to bring *The Princess and the Foal* to life.

Other books by Stacy Gregg

Pony Club Secrets series:

Mystic and the Midnight Ride

Blaze and the Dark Rider

Destiny and the Wild Horses

Stardust and the Daredevil Ponies

Comet and the Champion's Cup

Storm and the Silver Bridle

Fortune and the Golden Trophy

Victory and the All-Stars Academy

Flame and the Rebel Riders

Angel and the Flying Stallions

Liberty and the Dream Ride

Nightstorm and the Grand Slam

Issie and the Christmas Pony

Pony Club Rivals series:

The Auditions

Showjumpers

Riding Star

The Prize

www.stacygregg.co.uk

The Princess and the Foal

Stacy Gregg

HarperCollins *Children's Books*

First published in hardback in Great Britain by
HarperCollins *Children's Books* in 2013
HarperCollins *Children's Books* is a division of HarperCollins*Publishers* Ltd,
77-85 Fulham Palace Road, Hammersmith, London, W6 8JB

For Stacy's blog, competitions, interviews and more,
visit www.stacygregg.co.uk

The HarperCollins website address is: www.harpercollins.co.uk

1

ISBN 978-0-00-746902-4

Printed and bound in England by Clays Ltd, St Ives plc

Is it true you ask? And I say yes, especially the most extraordinary bits, they are the very truest of all.

To Her Royal Highness Princess Haya Bint Al Hussein, and to all the other princesses who dare to dream.

This book is a work of fiction, inspired by the early life of Her Royal Highness Princess Haya Bint Al Hussein. Any historical events, real people or real locales in this novel are portrayed fictitiously. Other names, characters and incidents are the product of the author's imagination and any resemblance to actual events or locales or persons living or dead is entirely coincidental.

Midnight, 23 August 1986

Hello, Mama,

I am underneath my blankets with a torch as I write this. I don't dare turn the lights on because Frances might see and know that I am awake, and the last person I want to deal with right now is Frances.

I should be asleep, but I am too full of nerves about tomorrow. Santi has a calendar in his office at the stables and I have marked off the squares in red pen one by one, the knot in my belly tightening as the day grows closer. For a long time it seemed forever away. And now suddenly there is no more waiting. In a few hours it will be dawn and I will go down to the stables and prepare Bree. I'll braid her tail and bandage her legs and then we will load the horses on to the truck and travel across the desert, bound on a journey that must end in either defeat or honour and glory for the Royal Stables.

I am trembling as I write these words to you and I tell myself that it is not fear, it is excitement. In all the history of the King's Cup there has never been a girl rider. But I am not just a girl. I am a Bedouin of the Hashemite clan and I was born to ride. Thousands of years ago the women of my tribe sat astride their horses in battle and fought side by side with men. Well, I do not want to fight – all I want to do is win.

A thousand faces will stare down from the grandstand tomorrow. Baba will watch me from the Royal Box with Ali by his side, and no doubt Frances will have elbowed her way in too. She'll be waiting for me to fail, to make a fool of myself in front of all those people. All the time undermining me to Baba, saying it is not right for the daughter of the King of Jordan to spend her time hanging around the stables, mucking out the dung. She is always trying to make me into something I am not.

Frances wants me to be like some princess in the storybooks – confined to my tower, dressed in ball gowns and a golden crown and glass slippers. I mean, who in their right mind would wear glass slippers? If I had my way, I would wear jodhpurs all day long.

"Your mother always deported herself as a gracious lady." That is exactly what Frances says. She talks so posh sometimes it is as if she is the royal one not just my governess.

Frances is always telling me I should be more like you. It is so annoying because if you were actually here then I wouldn't have to listen to her. I would be allowed to do as I like and I would never have to wear stupid dresses to dinner or put up with any of the rules that Frances makes up.

I tell her that you were a Queen, but you wore a T-shirt and jeans. I remember your favourite pair of red jeans. The ones you bought in Rome when you were very young, before you married Baba.

You wore those red jeans and your long hair was always loose over your shoulders and swept back off your face. I have grown my hair long now too, but it is plain brown. Baba insists that I look just like you, but you always looked like a movie star to me with your green eyes and dark blonde hair. If I close my eyes sometimes, I can see your face and hear your laughter like music filling the palace at Al Nadwa.

I remember I would ask you, "Can I become a Queen

one day?" and your answer was always the same. You would tell me, "Haya, you are a Princess of Jordan. Perhaps one day you will be a Queen, *Inshallah*. But remember your title is on a piece of paper, on a page of a history book, no more than that. It's what you have inside that means everything. You must always be yourself, Haya, never pretend. Do you understand?"

I would look at your face and you would be very serious, but then you would pick me up and smother me with kisses until I giggled and we would laugh together as you held me close in your arms.

The last time I asked you this question we were in the gardens at Al Nadwa. It was a summer day and you had spread a blanket on the lawn in the shade of the big pomegranate tree. Ali was there with us too, playing with his toys. At least I think Ali was there. Sometimes I wonder if I am making bits up. I am twelve now and that day has faded in my mind like an old photograph.

I have another memory and this one is very clear. We are outside Baba's office, you and me and Ali. You are kneeling down on the marble floor in front of Ali, grasping his tiny hands as he wobbles on his chubby little legs.

He steadies himself and then gently, carefully, you let him go. You keep your arms encircling him as Ali rocks back and forth, but he doesn't fall and you smile with delight and pick him up and say, "Oh, my darling Ali. Now that you can stand on your own feet I can leave you for a while."

Mama, I have been doing my best to stand up, to find my feet without you there to hold my hands. My two legs were not strong enough at first, but then Bree came along with four legs to carry us both. Her heart and courage gave me the strength that I needed.

I wish you could be there to see me ride her tomorrow. Baba says that if I have something important to tell you, I should write to you. But I could never do it. Not until tonight. I have so much to tell you, about me and Bree and everything that has happened since you've been gone. But it is very late and my hand is getting cramp. It is quite hard writing on a mattress when you are holding a torch in one hand and trying to breathe under the blankets. If you were here, you would tell me to finish the letter tomorrow and get some sleep.

Mama, you know how I said I wasn't afraid? Well, maybe I am, just a little. This is the greatest contest in the kingdom; what if Bree and I are not good enough?

I do not care that Frances and her supporters think it is wrong for a princess to ride. But I know how important this is to our people and I feel the weight of expectation upon me. When I ride into that arena, I carry their hopes along with me and I am determined that I will not let them down. I do this to make Baba proud, but also to prove myself, to show them that when I am on a horse I am the equal of any man.

I am a princess, but this is no fairy tale. If it were then I would know what is to come, my happy-ever-after. But I do not yet know how the story will end. All I know is that this story of me and Bree begins like fairy tales do:

Many years ago, once upon a time in Arabia...

Chapter 1

The Storm

Two lions stand guard at the entrance to the Royal Palace. They stand upright on all fours, alert and ready. Their powerful, sleek bodies are golden in the afternoon sun.

If the lions turned round, just a whisker, then they would see the little girl who stalks up silently behind them. But they do not move; their eyes stay trained on the stairs below.

The girl tiptoes forward in *one-two-three* quick strides. She has chosen her lion and in a bold leap she vaults up his rump and on to his back. Heart racing, she reaches out with both hands and grasps his mane tight and then she digs her tiny heels into the lion's flanks.

"Go!" she commands. "Go now!"

Leaning low over his mane, she kicks him on, the way she has seen her uncle ride his polo ponies. Just ten metres away there is a massive stone wall that borders the palace compound. If she can ride fast enough then the lion will leap the wall and they'll keep riding out across the green lawns of the Royal Court. Then beyond the next wall until the pink limestone buildings of Amman disappear and all that is left is the bleached, sunburnt sand of the Arabian desert. A lion can travel swiftly across the sand on his padded paws, but first they must leap the wall!

She is pressing the lion on, crouching low, legs kicking and arms pumping, when she senses a tall, dark shadow looming over her.

"Your Royal Highness."

The little girl looks up and smiles at the kindly face of Zuhair, head of the Royal Household Staff.

"Princess Haya," Zuhair says, "Queen Alia is looking for you."

Haya swings her leg over and then slides down the rump of the statue, landing neatly on her feet and running on ahead of Zuhair. She is three years old, with bright brown eyes and shoulder-length dark hair. Small for her age, her skinny arms are only just strong enough to push open the massive front doors of the palace that are made of heavy teak studded with brass orbs the size of her head.

In the hallway the portraits of Kings look down on her as she skips along, her feet pattering against the cool marble floor. She likes the way their eyes follow her as she runs by. Her father is King, but he is not on the wall. Whenever they have tried to hang his portrait, her Baba always says no thank you, he has no wish to stare at himself all day. He prefers photos of tanks and boats, and horses of course. Her Baba loves horses, just like Haya.

They call her father the Lion of Jordan, but Haya has never heard him roar. He is a soft-spoken man, handsome with short-cropped dark hair and a moustache. His dark eyes are bright with intelligence and his smile is gentle and kind.

But today, when Haya peeks in from the hallway through the door of his office, her Baba is not smiling. He sits at his desk, his brow furrowed deep with concern. In the centre of the office there is a large bearskin rug and her Mama is there too, standing on the bear and holding her little brother Ali on her hip.

"I have spoken to the officials in Tafilah," the Queen says. "Conditions there grow more desperate by the hour.

Refugees are pouring in. Many of them are women and children and they need food and medicine. The hospital staff are exhausted. There are no beds left. People are sleeping on floors and without blankets. They cannot wait another day. I should go there this afternoon in the helicopter and take them medicines and supplies while you meet with the foreign delegates in Aqaba."

Prince Ali squirms on the Queen's hip as she speaks. Only this afternoon he stood up for the first time and now he is reluctant to be restrained by his mother's arms any longer. His sturdy little legs kick out as he wriggles in a bid for freedom.

The worried expression does not leave the King's face at his wife's suggestion. "Alia, we agreed at breakfast that you would take the car. It is too dangerous to fly with a storm coming."

"If I take the helicopter then I can be home again by nightfall," the Queen says. And then before her husband can object she adds, "Badr Zaza has offered to fly me."

Badr Zaza is the King's own pilot and in all of Jordan there is no one better. The King nods in agreement at his wife's plan. "If Badr Zaza is willing to undertake the journey then I know you will be safe..."

"I want to come too."

It is Haya. She is standing in the doorway, eyes bright with excitement.

"Haya," her Mama cautions. "What did I say at dinner last night? I told you, if you wanted to come with me, you had to eat your steak and your Brussels sprouts."

"Ali didn't eat his either!" Haya offers as her defence.

"Ali is staying home too," her Mama says, rocking Haya's brother gently on her hip. "Grace will take care of you until I get home and next time, if you eat everything on your plate, then you may come with me, OK?"

There is a storm coming, but right now the sun still shines on the palace. On the lawn, not far from the pomegranate tree where Haya played that morning with her mother, a helicopter roosts like a sleeping dove.

"Are you going to fly away?" Haya asks her mother.

"Yes," the Queen says, "but Grace will look after you while I am gone."

Grace, their nanny, stands beside them on the balcony that leads to the lawn. She is holding Prince Ali in her arms. Grace is nice; she bakes biscuits.

Haya frowns. "Will you tuck me in?"

"Not tonight. Baba will be home in time to put you to bed and I will be there when you wake up in the morning."

Grace reaches out to take Haya's hand. It is time to say goodbye.

"Be good, Haya," her mother whispers in her ear as she bends down and kisses her.

The Queen kisses Ali too and then sets off across the lawn towards the helicopter.

"*Wait! Mama!*" Haya shouts, but the helicopter engine roars to life and drowns her words. Grace's hand is clasped firmly over hers, anchoring her to the balcony. Then suddenly Grace's hand is empty. Haya has broken free and is running helter-skelter after her mother across the flat, green lawn.

The Queen has almost reached the helicopter by the time the little princess catches up with her.

"*Mama!*" Haya's tiny hands clutch at the Queen's trouser leg. Startled, her mother looks down and sees Haya standing there beside her. Above their heads the blades of the helicopter begin to turn. The dove is waking.

Haya has something to tell her Mama, but her voice is too light as the engines of the helicopter thrum overhead. Her words are lost the moment they leave her lips. "*Don't go!*" she shouts. "*Stay with me. I love you, Mama.*" And then she looks up into her mother's eyes and Haya realises that she does not need to say anything because her mother understands.

The Queen bends down and picks up her daughter, taking her in her arms and hugging her tight. She kisses her one last time, and Haya feels the softness of Mama's skin. Then Grace is beside them and her mother is passing her over into the nanny's arms. Grace, who is still holding Ali, manages to straddle Haya on one hip and Ali on the other as she walks back to the garden terrace.

The helicopter blades turn slowly and then faster and faster until they are a blur. The wind gets stronger and whips at Haya's hair, flattens the flowers in the gardens below.

At first, the helicopter rocks up off the ground and bumps back down again as if it cannot make up its mind. Then, suddenly, it lifts up like a leaf caught by a gust of wind, rising straight into the air. It hovers for a moment and then arcs away, clearing the high palace walls and the tops of the trees beyond, setting a flight path towards the distant hills.

Haya tries to keep watching it, but the sun blinds her eyes. She shuts them tight, just for a moment, and when she opens them again, the helicopter is gone.

*

Haya curls herself up tightly into a ball. It is pitch-black in here, but nice and warm too, and she has her favourite toy, Doll, with the pink hat and sewn-on eyes and squishy cotton legs, with her for company.

"Shhhh," she whispers to Doll. "I can hear them coming. Be quiet now or they will find us."

There are voices outside and then car doors slamming. Haya feels her heart racing as the engine begins to purr. They are moving!

Uh-oh. The car has stopped again. There is the sound of voices once more and then footsteps, and suddenly the car boot is wide open and she is blinded by the glare of daylight.

"Haya! Not again!"

It is Baba. He has opened the car boot and found her!

"Haya." The King hardly seems surprised to see his daughter in the boot of the car. "Out you hop, please. I need to go now."

The first time Haya hid in the boot of Baba's Mercedes she made it all the way to Aqaba. But ever since then the King has been wise to her tricks and he always checks the car before he drives off.

Haya unfurls herself slowly and reluctantly, as if stalling for time will help matters.

"Please can I come?" she asks hopefully. "I won't be any trouble."

The King tries to suppress a smile at her antics as he bends down and lifts her out of the boot. "Somehow I find that very hard to believe."

Haya isn't going anywhere and so it is up to Grace to keep her amused. That afternoon they are baking biscuits in the palace kitchen. Grace makes them with dates and almonds and it is Haya's job to roll the mixture into little balls, dip them in sugar and then squish them down with a fork before they are put on the baking tray.

Ismail, the head chef, is grumpy that they are taking up his kitchen space. He doesn't complain – how can he tell off the daughter of a King? But he does clatter about, making extra loud noises banging his pots and pans as he cooks. He is making *mansef* for dinner: a rich dish of lamb with rice and thick pungent yoghurt. *Bedouin food*, Ismail calls it, one meal powerful enough to sustain you for many days.

This is what Haya's ancestors survived on during nomadic voyages across the great deserts. Her great-grandfather, King Abdullah, ate *mansef* with Lawrence of Arabia when he led the Bedouin army in the Arab Revolt.

Haya never met her great-grandfather, but she has seen his portrait on the wall of Kings. Baba was with him on the day that he died. He was accompanying his grandfather to pray, climbing the stairs of the mosque in Jerusalem, when an assassin opened fire. King Abdullah was shot and Haya's father would have been killed too if he had not worn his new uniform that day, with his medal for sword-fighting pinned over his heart. The medal stopped a bullet and saved her father's life.

Haya's father, Hussein, has been the King since he was seventeen years old. Presidents and prime ministers, kings and queens all come to Al Nadwa to meet him. They sit and talk for hours, but they never bring their children with them to play. It is all very, very dull as far as Haya is concerned.

During these visits there are grand dinners and the kitchen becomes a flurry of activity with six cooks working at once – so Haya cannot understand why Ismail is so grouchy about sharing his kitchen today. Surely there is enough space for her and Grace to bake biscuits alongside him?

When the biscuits are ready, they eat them in the Blue

Room. It is much smaller than the grand dining room and is just for family. Everything about it is very blue – blue walls, blue curtains, even blue plates and water glasses. Haya likes to pick the glasses up and look through them so her food is blue too.

No matter how busy her father is, he always eats breakfast with them, but often he does not make it home in time for dinner. Kings have a lot of work to do.

"Your father is the King of a nation," her Mama says. "The people of Jordan are all your brothers and sisters and we must love and care for them just like we care for you."

Haya has millions of brothers and sisters. But she mostly has Ali and there are only three places set at the dinner table that night for her and Ali and Grace because her Baba has not returned from Aqaba and Mama is still in Tafilah at the hospital. Usually at dinner everyone laughs and talks, but tonight it is quiet and Grace is acting very strangely as if she is anxious about something. Haya wonders if it has anything to do with the phone call that she took just before dinner.

There is a storm coming. Outside the windows of Haya's bedroom the tops of the palm trees are bending and swaying in the wind. When Grace puts Haya to bed she stays with her for a long time because the noises are quite scary – even when you are brave like Haya.

"I want to stay up until Baba and Mama get home," Haya says as Grace tucks her in. Haya's bedroom is upstairs and her bed is right beside the window. She likes to lie there and gaze up at the aeroplanes. The palace is so close to the airport that when the planes take off Haya thinks she could actually stick her hand out and touch their bellies. She likes to stare at the lights twinkling red, green and white on the tips of their wings as they fly overhead. But tonight there are no planes to watch. The winds are too strong and the airport has been closed.

Grace strokes her hair, then tucks Doll tightly into bed beside her. "Go to sleep. I will be in the room next door with Ali."

Haya squirms about to get comfy, wrestling with Doll beneath the blankets. She cannot sleep. The wind is howling now. Outside her window the palm trees are being shaken like rag dolls.

In the blackness of her bedroom, Haya clutches on to Doll. Fresh thunder rolls across the heavens and she is just about to call out for Grace when she hears the sound of voices, coming from downstairs. They are home!

Grasping Doll by the arm, Haya swings her legs over

the side of the bed and scampers across the landing.

As she comes down the stairs, she can see her father. He is home and he has company. The King is speaking to a man in uniform, one of the Royal Staff. The man has his head bowed as he hands an object to her father, something small and shiny.

"*Baba!*"

Haya dashes down the staircase. The King turns to see the little princess in her pyjamas, clutching a dolly with a pink hat, and that is when Haya realises with shock that he is crying.

Haya has never seen her father cry before. He weeps openly, letting the tears run down his cheeks without trying to wipe them away.

"Haya." Her Baba picks her up and his arms feel strong and safe around her. "It's OK…"

Haya hugs him tight and buries her face in his chest, but as she does so, she catches a glimpse of the object that he cradles in his right hand. The small and shiny thing that the man passed to him. Haya can see now what it is.

The shattered remains of her Mama's wristwatch.

CHAPTER 2

The Legend of Al Khamseh

Baba cradles Haya as she sobs. She cries so hard, the tears threaten to choke her and she cannot breathe. She clings to Baba, and his arms are strong as he holds her tight and close, and yet it is not enough to comfort her. She wants her Mama. But her Mama is not coming home. Not tonight. Not ever again.

This is what Baba has told Haya. He said that Mama was very brave to go to Tafilah, knowing that the storm was coming. She helped the people in the hospital, gave them blankets and medicine and food. The skies were black when they left the hospital, but the pilot hoped they might outrun the thunderclouds. They were high above the desert on the outskirts of Amman when the storm caught up to them and lightning struck the helicopter.

That night Haya does not leave her Baba's side. Even when Baba has to go on the radio and tell the whole country that the Queen has died, he keeps her close to him. She sits on his lap as he writes the words that he will say to the nation. When he speaks on the radio, a soft, fuzzy noise can be heard in the background. It is the sound of Ali's breath drawing in and out as he dozes peacefully in the King's arms.

That night Haya sleeps with Ali in the big bed with Baba. When she wakes up, the storm is gone. And so is Mama.

At first, she does not truly believe it. Any moment now, Haya expects Mama to walk in, with her arms open wide, her voice lilting and musical as she calls out Haya's name.

She will come back, Haya thinks. *She cannot really be gone.*

But there is no Mama at breakfast or to brush her hair or choose her clothes, and Ali will not stop crying. He cries because he does not understand why Mama won't come to him.

"Shhh, Ali, it's me. I am here." Haya lowers the rail on the cot and climbs in beside her brother. Ali's tiny face is streaked with tears and his little hands clutch tightly on to his blanket. Haya lies down with him and holds him until he stops crying.

By dinnertime, Haya has decided that it is all her fault. She is the reason that Mama is gone, but it is OK because she can fix it. That night, when her meal is served, she eats all her meat. She almost gags as she chews the steak, but she cleans her plate and she is pleased with herself. That will do the trick. Now Mama will come back.

But the meat doesn't work. And even the next night when she eats her meat all up again, plus Brussels sprouts as well, there is still no Mama. Haya is beginning to think that no matter how much meat she eats, Mama will not come home. By the third night, Haya pushes her plate aside and stares at the steak as if it now silently carries the blame. She will never eat it again.

Every night Baba stays at her bedside and strokes her hair until she sleeps, but he cannot stop the nightmares that wake her, leaving her alone in the darkness, sobbing. They are nightmares about her Mama in the storm. Haya sees the moment when the lightning struck. Was Mama afraid when she fell from the sky? Did it hurt?

In the first days after the crash the palace was stunned into silence. Now it becomes noisy as the whirl of preparations begin for the state funeral. Dignitaries from across Arabia and around the world come to pay their respects. Haya's aunts and cousins are so very kind to Haya and Ali; in a strange way it is almost like a party with everyone here together. And then suddenly everyone is gone once more and the palace feels cold and empty without Mama's laughter.

Haya's footsteps echo through the corridors. The palace has changed. She tries to bake biscuits like she used to, but it is weird how Ismail never, ever gets cross, even when she is in his way. He keeps looking at Haya, his eyes misty, as if he is about to cry. There is so much sorrow here that Haya cannot stand it.

"It's OK," Baba says. "I know a place where we can go."

When the Mercedes arrives, Grace, Haya and Ali pile into the back seat and the King sits upfront with his bodyguard as they cruise out of the palace gates into the grounds of the Royal Compound.

There is a checkpoint at the edge of the compound and their driver pulls over to speak to the guards at the gate. The guards salute and wave them on and very soon they have left the compound and the suburbs of Amman behind them and they are climbing the hills into the forest. The road twists and winds through the pine trees. It is a hot day, but inside the air-conditioned car they are cool.

Grace tries to talk, but Haya turns her head away and stares out at the tree shadows flickering shafts of sunlight on the tinted windows, her thoughts lost in the woods. She has no words left. She does not want to talk, not about anything and especially not about Mama.

At the crest of the hill there is a pair of white posts with bright blue wrought-iron gates. The car turns here and there are tall palm trees bordering the driveway on both sides, and ahead of them the whitewashed buildings of Al Hummar, the Royal Stables.

The stables look like a white Spanish castle, the doors and windows trimmed in bright blue paint. Brilliant red flowers spill out of terracotta pots and purple vines climb the archways that lead through to the stables. There are two courtyards, and in the first of these is a drinking pool with blue painted tiles and a fountain in the middle so the horses can pause in the yard each day to take their fill. The ground around the fountain is hard as rock, baked by the sun and worn smooth by horses' hooves. The only thing that grows here is an ancient grey-green olive tree, its twisted boughs providing shade in the heat of the day.

Around the edge of both courtyards are the loose boxes, hidden beneath the shade of Spanish arches. And inside the loose boxes are horses.

The horses at Al Hummar are the most beautiful in all of Arabia. To Haya they are enchanted creatures, with silken manes, muzzles soft as velvet and dark eyes that can see into her soul.

There are fifty horses here and all are pure-bred Arabian. Santi is in charge of Al Hummar. His real name is Mr Santiago Lopez and he built these stables for Haya's father, modelling them on his own back home in Spain. There is always music pouring out of Santi's office in the first courtyard. "It makes the horses want to dance," Santi says and Haya is not sure whether to believe him or not.

Titch. That is what Santi calls her and now he says, "Ah, Titch, thank goodness you have arrived. The horses have been asking me all morning when you would come!"

Haya does not say a word, but Santi is undaunted by her silence.

"You talk too much, Titch!" he tells her. "Be quiet, little one, you will scare the horses with all your noise!"

And Haya cannot help but smile just a little bit. Santi

does not fuss over her the way they do at the palace. He does not look at her as if she is an object of pity. He leaves her to roam the stable yards as he talks with the King while Grace sits in the sunshine with Ali asleep, cradled in her arms.

Santi always has a pot of hot cardamom coffee on the hotplate beside his desk. He pours a cup for the King and Grace and puts the needle down on the record player, the strains of Spanish music filling the courtyard.

They sit outside the office and watch the young fillies gather at the water trough like a group of girls sharing secrets. When these fillies with their slender, dainty legs like ballerinas grow up, the rose-grey dapples on their rumps will fade and they will be pure white, like their mothers who stand in the shade of the loose boxes watching over them.

The mares, fillies, colts and stallions all live together. Haya knows most of them by name and she makes her rounds to say hello. She is too little to look over the doors, so she has to climb up to see inside the loose boxes, hanging on to the wooden rails as she pays each horse a visit.

Of course she has her favourites. There is the chestnut mare Jamila who looks like a seahorse with flared nostrils and a wide forehead. Jamila has a pretty white blaze and a golden mane that hangs down all the way past her shoulders. She has won many ribbons and rosettes because of her beauty. Beside Jamila is Bahar, an elegant, freckled grey stallion with enormous brown eyes rimmed with long black lashes that flutter like a movie star. Bahar is aloof, he does not always want to say hello, but Haya persists, holding out a handful of alfalfa until he finally deigns to take it from her.

The last box that Haya visits is that of her most favourite of all, a mare named Amina.

Amina's box is down the driveway in the second courtyard. She is a bay mare, with a deep red coat and lustrous jet-black mane. Black stockings run up her legs all the way to her hocks.

Most Arabians have delicate muzzles, but Amina's nose is not so pretty. She is a Desert Born Arab, with coarser features, a flatter profile and heavier jaw. Amina is built to jump. She is one of the best jumpers in the stables; fast and fearless.

Whenever Haya comes to the stables, she always asks Santi if she can ride her and he always shakes his head saying, "Amina is powerful and highly-strung, too much horse for a little Titch like you."

"I'm not little," Haya tries to argue.

But Santi is firm. "You can have a lesson on Dandy," he says.

Haya doesn't want Dandy. He is an ill-tempered Shetland gelding with short legs and a bushy mane. He is so little Haya can brush him without using the orange crate to stand on. He tries to bite her when she brushes his flank. He is not the horse for her.

*

One day they visit Al Hummar, just Haya, Grace and Ali. Haya has been coming here every week since Mama died and now she is almost four. Santi is there at the gates as always to welcome them and takes Grace to his office and pours her a coffee while Ali pulls out a record to hand to Santi and Haya takes herself off to visit the horses.

Today she makes her way directly to the second courtyard to see Amina.

Amina's head is already poking out over the loose-box door, her dainty ears swivelling attentively at the sound of Haya's approaching footsteps. Santi has left the old orange crate beside Amina's box for her and Haya props it up against the door, climbing on top of it so that she is tall enough to see inside.

"Amina!"

The mare nickers in reply and nuzzles her. Haya usually feeds the horses with handfuls of alfalfa, but today she has brought Amina something special. She digs into her pocket and pulls out three round white peppermints. Teetering on the orange crate, she extends her hand out flat with the offering and the mare eagerly snuffles her palm, nibbling daintily, brushing her skin with soft lips until all three peppermints have vanished. Haya giggles as Amina's mouth works furiously, tasting the mints. The mare begins to jiggle her head up and down, her eyes going wide as she chews. Haya's tiny hands work the bolts on the loose-box door.

Haya climbs up the stable door and this time when she reaches the top rung she throws herself into the air! Amina sidesteps as she feels Haya's weight land on her back. She gives a snort as Haya begins to tap her with her heels, urging her on like the stone lions at Al Nadwa.

Amina is not cold like the stone lions; her body feels warm between Haya's bare legs. Haya taps again with her heels and pulls on the guide rope she has strung round Amina's neck and they set off up the driveway towards the main courtyard.

As they enter the courtyard, other horses stick their

heads out over the stable doors to nicker their greetings. Amina is a confident mare and without a glance at the other horses she walks straight up to the fountain and shoves her muzzle deep into the cool trough. Up on her back, Haya is chatting away to the mare, swinging her legs back and forth as Amina snorts and flicks at the water.

Suddenly the door to Santi's office flies open. Grace is there, looking very anxious. "Haya!" she cries out. She is about to race towards the fountain when Santi grabs her arm.

"She's OK," Haya hears him say. "They have made it this far. The mare will not hurt her. Come back and finish your coffee and leave them both a while longer."

In the car on the way home Haya is no longer silent. She is full of her adventure, already making plans to ride Amina the next time she returns to Al Hummar.

"We shall see," Grace says, trying to be firm, but so relieved to see the Princess smiling and laughing that she does not say no.

That night, when Baba arrives home, Haya cannot wait to tell him.

"I rode Amina today," she says as she clambers into bed with Doll under her arm.

Her father raises an eyebrow in surprise. "Did you really?"

"Santi says I am a natural," Haya says proudly. And then she asks, "What is a natural?"

Baba smiles. "Horses are in your blood, Haya. For many generations the Bedouin have bred the best horses. The Arabians in our stables can be traced back to the first horses, the five mares of Al Khamseh."

Haya knows the Legend of Al Khamseh. Her father has told it to her lots of times before, but she wants it again. She lies back on the pillow and her father tucks the blankets tight around her before he begins.

"Two thousand years ago your ancestor, Mohammad, Peace Be Upon Him, wanted to create the perfect horse, one with the stamina, speed, courage and loyalty to carry him across the great deserts. So he gathered together a hundred of his very best mares and set a test. For three long days he kept the horses under the hot desert sun, penned without food or drink to test their stamina. Then he released the mares, and let them gallop to the waterhole of a distant oasis.

"The mares galloped on, closer and closer to the oasis. Then, just when they had almost reached the water's edge, he raised his battle horn to his lips and blew, calling the mares back to him once more.

"Of the hundred mares, only five were courageous and loyal enough to turn round and return to his side. These mares became known as 'The Five'. Each of them was a different colour – a grey, a black, a roan, a chestnut and a bay. It is said that their noble blood is in the veins of every true Bedouin Arabian."

"Why was it only mares?" Haya asks. "Weren't there stallions too?"

"Oh, yes, there were a great many stallions," her father says. "But to the Bedouin it is the mothers – the mares – who matter the most."

"Did Mohammad, Peace Be Upon Him, have a favourite mare?" Haya asks.

"They say that he loved the bay best of all," her father replies.

"Amina is a bay," Haya says. She is quiet for a moment and then she asks, "Do camels have noble blood?"

Her father smiles again. "Camels are magnificent creatures. Without them, the Bedouin could not have conquered the great desert. But horses are bonded to us, deep in our hearts. In the desert, a Bedouin will leave his camels outside his tent, but his horse sleeps with him inside, kept safe by his bed."

"I want to do that," Haya says. "I wish Amina could come here and sleep in my bedroom with me."

"I think Amina might prefer her loose box," her father says. "And I don't think Zuhair would be very pleased to see hoofprints on the carpets."

The King tucks Haya in more tightly and strokes her hair. "Sleep well, my Bedouin Princess."

That night, for the first time in ages, Haya does not cry. She lies back on her pillow and stares at the stars, imagining galloping on Amina. She can hear the battle horn and feel the surge of the mare's speed, as she grips on tight with her legs, spurring Amina forward. Bare skin against silky fur, the coarse rope of the mare's mane tangled in her hands and Amina's wonderful, warm, sweet smell filling Haya's senses as she drifts off to sleep.

Chapter 3

Aqaba

One morning at breakfast Haya's father tells her that Grace is leaving.

"Grace's mother is very sick," the King explains, "and there is no one else to care for her. Grace needs to go home."

Grace's mother lives a long way from Amman so Grace cannot stay at the palace to look after Haya and Ali.

"Will the new nanny bake biscuits?" Haya asks Grace.

Grace smiles. "I am sure she will."

"But how will she know how I like them?" Haya asks.

Grace gives Haya a hug and wipes the tears off her hot little cheeks. "Perhaps she will make them differently," she tells Haya, "but I am sure you will like her biscuits too."

She cuddles Haya close. "Your new nanny will love you as much as I do," Grace whispers softly. "Wait and see."

*

On the day that Grace goes away forever, the King takes Haya and Ali to the Summer House in Aqaba. They set off, just the three of them, in the blue sports car, all alone – except for the bodyguards who travel in two separate cars, one in front and one behind.

They honk and beep their way through the narrow streets of the market district where merchants hang their stalls with colourful rugs and scarves, and soon leave the creamy white apartment blocks of the city behind. Now there are clusters of houses amid bare hills, their flat rooftops trimmed with satellite dishes. Shaggy brown goats wander loose by the roads where camel herders live in tents constructed out of brightly coloured blankets, ignoring the motorways of traffic whizzing by them.

On the open highway horns blast and lorries thunder past the little sports car, but Haya's father is not flustered, weaving and zipping in between them. At one point he overtakes his bodyguards and Haya looks back through the rear window to see the two black Mercedes struggling to keep up as her father takes the bends at top speed.

The roads climb higher until they finally crest the ridge and see desert mountains stretching out to the horizon. The mountains are the colour of rust, but the soil beside the road is chalky pale and the only plants that grow here are thorn bushes.

Haya can feel her ears about to pop as they descend the mountain roads to a flat stretch of highway that goes all the way to Aqaba, where desert sand at last meets sea.

The Summer House is very simple compared to their palace, sunny and bright with a view over the sea and doors that open out on to the beach. Haya remembers summer days spent here, always in her swimming costume with her feet covered in sand.

The members of the King's Guard have arrived ahead of them to check that everything is as it should be, and the housekeeper and chef are preparing lunch. Haya and Ali just have time for a swim before the food is ready. It is a feast of ripe tomatoes and hummus and baba ghanoush and tabbouleh, and a dish called upside down, made with aubergines. Haya shows her father shells that she found on the beach after her swim. Her favourite is a white one shaped in a twist like an ice-cream cone.

In the afternoon, Haya takes Ali for a walk in the garden and holds him up to grasp the oranges that grow there and pluck them from the trees.

As she walks back into the kitchen with her arms full of oranges, Haya is about to call out for Mama, expecting her to be here waiting for her, just like she used to be. Then the words choke in her throat as she remembers all of a sudden and the oranges tumble to the floor.

On the drive home the next day Haya is silent. She stares out of the window while her father tells her about Frances. She will be Haya's new nanny and is arriving tomorrow.

"Frances will live with us just like Grace did," her father explains.

Haya has never had a new nanny. She keeps looking out of the window as her father tells her how wonderful Frances will be. Haya can taste her tears, salty like the waves at Aqaba.

*

"There she is, Ali, you see?" Haya lifts her little brother up to the window so that he can see Frances getting out of her car and walking to the front door. "That's her," Haya tells him. "She's going to be really nice and love us like Grace did. Grace promised."

All Haya can see is the top of her head, the auburn hair twisted up into a sleekly groomed beehive. Frances is wearing a navy blue cotton piqué dress and the stiff pleats of her skirt stick out around her. As she walks up the front steps, the two stone lions on either side of the door don't move. *They wouldn't bother to eat you*, Haya thinks. Frances looks very bony, not enough meat for them.

The King is very lucky to have secured Frances's services at such short notice. Frances has, until recently, been in the service of a family in Zurich where she mixed with a very international set. She can speak English and French, *bien sûr*, and a little German, but not Arabic so do not even ask her to try. She has worked for the very best people, *the cream of society*. Haya knows this because she hears Frances telling Zuhair as she walks down the corridors of Al Nadwa, her sensible heels clacking on the marble floors.

Frances informs Zuhair that she is a governess which is altogether different to a nanny and he will please address her as Miss Ramsmead. She explains how she likes her tea: with milk, no lemon, no sugar. The tea itself needs to be brewed for exactly two minutes, no more, no less, and she would like a cup of it right now, please, brought up to her room.

Haya, who has been listening and watching from the upstairs landing, has to duck hastily into her bedroom as Frances breezes straight upstairs ahead of Zuhair.

After a quick glance round Grace's old room, she pronounces it "adequate" and tells Zuhair he may fetch her suitcases and the tea now.

Zuhair is not used to being spoken to in this manner. Even the Queen never spoke to him like this. But his face does not show a flicker of expression as he says, "Certainly, Miss Ramsmead," and heads downstairs to get her bags and explain to the kitchen staff the special requirements of the new governess.

Haya is staring at Frances while she rummages distractedly in her handbag, but suddenly her new governess stops and swivels her head round. The Princess ducks behind the door, but it is too late.

"Good afternoon. You must be Her Royal Highness Princess Haya?"

Haya stays hidden behind the door.

Frances sighs. "It is not good manners for a Princess to greet someone like this," she says. "The correct thing would be to present yourself as I am doing now. I am Miss Ramsmead, but you may call me Frances if you wish."

She stands expectantly, waiting for Haya to emerge. When at last the Princess steps out on to the landing, Frances's eyes widen as she takes in dirty shorts, T-shirt and bare feet.

"You look more like a pauper's son than a King's daughter," she says.

Haya doesn't like to wear dresses – they get in the way when you are playing. She likes to wear shorts, just like Ali. But she has long dark hair to her shoulders and no one else has ever mistaken her for a boy before.

Frances inspects her, looking her up and down, and Haya is suddenly aware that she has not brushed her hair today and she did not have anyone to give her a bath after returning from the trip to the summer house.

"Your previous nanny clearly wasn't a suitable influence," Frances says and Haya feels her cheeks go hot. It is the way Frances says it – like Haya is not standing right there in front of her, as if she cannot hear what Frances is saying!

"Is this your room?" Frances gestures over Haya's shoulder. She walks straight past Haya and into her bedroom. Frances casts a glance around, and spies the photo of Haya and her mother on the dresser.

"I was an acquaintance of Queen Alia, did you know that?" she asks. She holds the picture frame in her hands and Haya has to control the urge to snatch it back from her.

"We met on more than one occasion in Europe," Frances continues, still holding the picture. "Before you were born, before she married your father. I thought to myself, now there is a young girl from a good family who will go far. Your mother was the epitome of grace, so beautiful…" As she says this, Frances's eyes lock on Haya's legs. She is staring at the grass-stained knees poking out of Haya's shorts.

"My poor girl," Frances tuts. "The state of you." She takes a deep breath. "Don't worry, things will change now that I am here."

She looks at her watch. "Now what time do you usually begin your lessons?"

"Lessons?"

"Yes," Frances says. "You know, your studies?"

Haya doesn't understand. She is only five. Surely that is too young for anything except playing?

At that moment one of the kitchen staff turns up

carrying a silver tray with a pot, cup and saucer and a jug of milk. "Tea, Miss Ramsmead," he says.

Frances lifts the jug with great suspicion, feeling it in her hands. "This milk is warm?"

He nods vigorously. "Yes! Hot milk."

Frances wrinkles her nose. "Tea requires cold milk," she says. The kitchen boy stares blankly at the tray that he has set down on the table.

"Well?" Frances says. "Take it away and bring me cold milk."

He rushes forward, grasps the milk jug and backs away nervously. Then he turns and dashes back down the stairs. Frances shakes her head as she watches him go and then looks back at Haya.

"I can see I will have my work cut out for me," she says.

Chapter 4

The Treasure Box

It doesn't take Haya long to figure out that Frances is two different people. There is Frances the Governess – all sour, thin-lipped and taut as piano wire. And then there is the other Frances, the one the King gets to see. Haya and Ali call her 'Happy Frances'.

Happy Frances will cheerfully play games and sing songs. She will sew the pink hat back on Doll just like Haya has been begging her to do for days. Happy Frances reads proper bedtime stories instead of ones that last just one page.

If the King is in the room then Happy Frances fusses over Haya and smothers her with cuddles. But her arms are so bony and her hugs are stiff and awkward. All they do is make Haya miss Grace more than ever.

Haya never talks to Baba about how much she misses Grace, just as she never speaks about how much she aches every single day for her Mama.

One day, Haya hears noises in the upstairs bedrooms, and walks in to find Frances overseeing her staff as they work their way through room by room with three large cardboard boxes.

Haya watches in horror as Frances picks up one of Mama's silk scarves and flings it into a box.

"What are you doing?"

Frances does not turn to look at her. "Decluttering."

"Those are Mama's things!" Haya can feel her cheeks turning hot. "You leave them alone!"

Frances shakes her head. "This is a palace, not a shrine. If you were more considerate, you would see that your father needs to put the past aside and move on."

If Baba were here then Haya would run to him right now – but he is away in Aqaba and Frances has chosen her moment all too well. Haya has no choice but to stand by helplessly as she watches Frances sweep her mother's memory away as if it were so much house dust.

No more Mama. That is the rule now that Frances is here.

There is a hole. Haya can feel it inside her, an emptiness that overwhelms her. Into this void she pushes down all thoughts of Mama. Only she does this a little too well, pushes too far.

Now, if she tries to picture her Mama's face or the sound of her voice, she finds it harder and harder. She is losing her Mama all over again. This time it is like Haya is trying to grab at smoke with her fingers. She wants so badly to hold on to her memories and yet her eyes well with tears whenever anyone mentions her Mama. And so people stop talking about the Queen in front of the little Princess. Everyone stops talking about Mama. Everyone, that is, except for the one person who should.

Frances barely met Queen Alia, but she speaks of her with an air of absolute authority.

"*Your mother would never…*" Frances always begins her lectures with these words and very soon Haya can hear them coming before Frances even opens her mouth. *Your mother would never…* dress like a boy, laugh too loud, get dirty fingernails, stain her clothes, forget to brush her hair, play childish games, or – worst of all – waste time with smelly, filthy horses.

Frances is an expert on the King too. She says His Majesty would be so much happier if Haya would try to be more feminine. "Your mother had such noble manners, she was such a lady."

A lady? Is that what Baba wants Haya to be? He has never mentioned it, but Frances says it over and over again, so Haya doesn't know any more. And she doesn't know how to tell her father about the dark empty place inside her that is getting bigger every day. When her Baba says, "You are very quiet, Haya, tell me what is wrong?" she finds that there are no words for her sadness and so she says, "It's nothing. I am fine."

Haya cannot voice her emotions, not even to Baba. But she has found a place to put them. They are kept inside her treasure box. The treasure box is made of gold. Well, not really: it is made of cardboard, a shoebox painted gold with magazine pictures stuck all over it. Kept safe inside, where no one else can see, Haya stores her most precious things: her memories of Mama and life before Frances came to the palace.

The box is her museum and Haya treats each item inside it with the utmost care. There is a pair of her Mama's sunglasses with tortoiseshell rims, huge and square like a TV set. Two tape cassettes – Abba and Gloria Gaynor – which she found with the glasses in the glove box of Mama's car after she died. A pink pebble from the beach at Aqaba and the pointy white ice-cream seashell, pressed flowers, wild blooms from the meadows near the Summer House, once soft and delicate, now brittle like parchment, tucked between the pages of a notebook. There are photographs too and empty bullet cartridges, made of cold metal, just like the ones that bounced off her father's medal.

Haya spends hours arranging everything from the treasure box on her bed and then packing it away again. The last item she puts in the box is an almost empty bottle of her mother's favourite perfume. Before she puts the bottle back she very carefully removes the stopper and dabs the tiniest amount on her wrist, just like her mother did. Then she closes her eyes and inhales deep breaths, until the scent overpowers all her other senses and the world disappears.

*

Several weeks after Frances arrives, with great reluctance, the governess gives in to Haya's pleading and they make a visit to the Royal Stables.

As usual, Santi is there to greet them when the car pulls up at Al Hummar.

"Welcome back, Titch!" He smiles at Haya. "The horses have missed you!"

Santi invites them into his office, where the music is playing and the pot of cardamom coffee is bubbling.

He offers Frances a cup. She takes a sip and then screws up her thin lips in disgust, placing the cup promptly on the table. "I should like a tour of the grounds, Señor Lopez."

Santi is very proud of his stables. He has given many tours here; Sultans and Kings have come to visit. None of them were ever as critical as Frances. The governess inspects the horses in the same way that she ran her eyes over Haya the day they met. "They're a little underweight, aren't they?"

"They are Arabians," Santi replies. "The breed is much lighter in the frame than the horses you are accustomed to back home in England."

"I know my breeds, Señor Lopez," Frances says. "All the same, I should like to see them a little more filled out than this."

"I did not realise that you were such a horsewoman, Miss Ramsmead," Santi says, casting a glance at Haya.

"Oh, yes," Frances says. "In England I rode with The Quorn. Have you heard of it?"

Santi raises an eyebrow. "That is a very exclusive hunt," he says. Frances looks smug until he adds, "You must know my wife Ursula. She hunted with them for many years. I will ask if she remembers you…"

"Oh," Frances falters. "Please don't bother. I never… rode to hounds very often. Besides, it was such a long time ago I hardly think—"

Suddenly a muzzle thrusts over the door of the loose box beside Frances. She emits a piercing shriek and leaps forward, almost landing on top of Haya.

"It's all right," Santi says as he reaches out to stroke the bay mare who has popped her head over the door. "This is Amina. She is being friendly; she didn't mean to scare you."

"I wasn't scared!" But Frances won't step any closer to the mare.

"She's got a rather coarse look about her for a pure-bred, hasn't she?" Frances says, glaring at Amina's flat nose and heavy jaw.

"Amina is Desert Born," Santi says. "Her temperament is excellent and she was once a very good showjumper…"

"Arabs don't jump," Frances says emphatically.

"That is what they say," Santi agrees, "but some, like Amina, are very bold, confident jumpers…"

"Yes, well, thank you, Señor Lopez," Frances says flatly. "I think we'll be leaving now."

"But we only just got here!" Haya says.

"I think we've been here quite long enough," Frances says. She walks back towards the car and Haya only just has enough time to snatch up a handful of alfalfa to feed to Amina.

"I wish you had tried to bite her," Haya whispers. "She deserves it."

Amina nickers. "I know," Haya agrees with the mare. "I don't think she does like you. And I don't think she likes me either."

"Stay for lunch!" Santi implores as Frances ushers Haya into the car. "Ursula can bring food up from the house for us."

"No, thank you."

"Well then, leave Titch here for the afternoon. She loves the horses and my grooms will keep a close eye on her."

"The grooms? She's not a horse!" Frances replies. "Thank you for the tour, Señor Lopez."

The car trip home is awful. "Those horses are ill-mannered brutes!" Frances proclaims. "Small wonder with Señor Lopez in charge! The dust and the dung in those yards…"

"I like it there." Haya juts her jaw out bravely. What is

wrong with dung anyway? To say there is dung in a horse yard is like saying there is sand in the desert.

The rest of the journey home is spent in silence. But the next day, when Haya asks to go to the stables, Frances says she can't. She has a piano lesson instead. And the piano lesson is followed by French and then ballet. There is no time for the stables.

*

"Baba? I don't feel so good."

The King puts down his newspaper and looks at his daughter. Haya's face is flushed and she has hardly touched her breakfast.

"You haven't got a fever," the King says as he feels her forehead.

"Maybe I am coming down with something?" Haya says hopefully.

"Maybe." Her father looks at her knowingly.

"Frances?" The King summons the governess. "Princess Haya will be coming with me today."

Haya packs her colouring-in pencils and waits with Doll at the front door as the driver brings the car round. She tries not to look too happy or too healthy as she gets in the back seat beside her father. The car cruises out of the gates and up the winding roads of the palace compound to the Royal Court.

"Welcome, Your Royal Highness!" The women who run the office are always pleased to see her. Her father's secretary brings the King his morning coffee and also some orange juice and crackers for Haya, with a stack of paper and more coloured pens. In the corner of the office Haya makes herself a fort out of sofa cushions and lies on the rug, drawing pictures of horses while her father talks on the phone and looks at the important papers on his desk.

She is very quiet when the King's ministers come for a meeting at the large polished-oak table in the corner of the room. Haya focuses hard on her colouring-in, but she hears them, their voices deep and serious as they discuss Egypt and Israel and a place called Camp David. After the men are gone, the King asks his secretary for more orange juice and chocolate biscuits. Then he takes off his shoes and climbs inside Haya's sofa-cushion fortress.

"Haya, are you feeling better now?"

"Yes, Baba."

"You are very quiet. Why don't you tell me what is wrong?"

Haya hesitates. She doesn't want to bother her father. He is a King with the weight of a nation on his shoulders.

"It's OK," her father says, "you can tell me."

"Frances won't take me to see the horses," Haya says. "I keep asking, but she always says no."

A misunderstanding. That is what Happy Frances calls it. Of course she is more than happy to escort the Princess to Al Hummar if that is what she wishes.

Haya is triumphant as they drive to the stables. Frances, meanwhile, has a face like poison. When they arrive, she refuses Santi's offer of coffee and returns to sit in the car while Haya visits the horses.

For two hours Frances just sits there, reading a romance novel. On the car trip home Frances stuffs the book in her handbag, but she still doesn't speak to Haya.

For the next fortnight visits to Al Hummar continue in this way. And then, one afternoon, the driver arrives at the front door of the palace to transport them to the stables and Haya notices that Frances isn't holding her handbag.

"Señor Lopez and I have had words," Frances says, and Haya is filled with despair until she adds, "he has agreed that there is no need for me to accompany you to the stables. It is more sensible for him to take care of you in the afternoons."

As Haya travels to the stables, she feels electrified with a sense of freedom. Frances has finally admitted defeat. Haya is going to Al Hummar stables on her own!

There are fifty horses to care for and a half-dozen grooms under Santi's command, but he is never too busy to spend time with Haya and is always waiting at the gates to greet her.

"I hope you are feeling strong, Titch," he says. "There is much work to do."

At the yards Yusef, the head groom, finds a pitchfork that is small enough for Haya's little hands and she follows along behind the two men to help with the chores. There are boxes to be mucked out first. She digs out the damp straw with her pitchfork and helps to throw down fresh bedding into the stalls. Then she fills the hayracks in each box with armfuls of lush green alfalfa.

In the boiling room she helps the groom, Radi, to stir the barley pot, a huge cast-iron cauldron strung up by metal chains on a hook over the fire. She is not allowed to touch the pot because it is very hot, but Radi lets her scoop up dry barley and add it to the water. Barley must boil for at least two hours, but Radi likes it to boil overnight. The horses, he says, have delicate bellies.

In the tack room, Haya has her own named hook and

a little bag of grooming brushes that Santi has made up for her: a hoof pick, a mane comb, a dandy brush and a curry comb. She takes her kit and goes from box to box, brushing the horses in turn, always saving her favourites till last. Amina's coat is growing thicker and fluffier. Winter is coming.

When the first snowfall comes and there are deep flurries in the courtyard, Haya clips a lead rope to Amina's halter and takes her out of the loose box. Amina shies at the snow, refusing to step in it, but Haya keeps coaxing her forward until the mare sticks a tentative hoof into the white crust. Then she dances forward, head held high, snorting and shaking her jet-black mane. Each snort creates a plume of sweet, shimmering steam in the cold morning air.

The snow begins to fall more heavily and Amina doesn't like the feeling of the flakes on her face. She buries her head in Haya's coat, trying to wipe the snow off. Haya laughs and takes Amina back to her loose box and then mixes her warm barley and chaff for supper.

*

As the season passes, Amina's winter coat begins to shed, slowly at first and then in great clumps as the weather gets warmer. Haya grooms her with a curry comb, exposing her glossy, sleek summer coat underneath. But the spring also reveals something more. Amina is changing in front of Haya's eyes, and she must tell Santi.

"There is a problem with Amina," Haya says, trying to adopt the tone that she's heard him use with his grooms. "I think she is getting too much barley. She is becoming very fat."

Santi laughs. "That mare is not fat, Titch, she is in foal."

*

That night, when the King is tucking her into bed, Haya tells him the good news.

"Amina is having a baby," she informs Baba. "She is very fat so it must be soon. Santi says I can watch her foal being born – if you say yes."

Her father considers this. "I'll talk to Santi. We'll pack a bag full of clothes and a torch and leave it ready in your bedroom. Foals are often born in the middle of the night so you will need to be organised to go at a moment's notice."

"But if it is at night, I'll be asleep!" Haya worries. "Will you wake me up?"

"I promise," the King says.

"Baba, do you love horses?"

"Yes, Haya."

"Did Mama love horses too?"

"She loved all animals," the King says.

"Did she ride horses like you do?"

"She rode," the King says, "and she loved sports. Your mother was a champion waterskier."

"I am going to be a champion too," Haya says. "I'm going to be a champion horse rider. One day I will ride in the King's Cup!"

It is a bold claim to make. The King's Cup is the most glorious sporting event in the whole of Jordan. Haya remembers Baba taking her with Mama and Ali to sit in the Royal Box and watch the horsemen compete. She remembers the banners waving, the heat of the sun and the noise of the crowds. And riders, on the most beautiful horses she had ever seen. The horsemen vaulted off their galloping Arabians, riding like daredevils. *One day*, she thought, *I will ride like them.*

"Champions need to get their sleep," the King tells her. "Especially five-year-old champions."

"I am nearly six," Haya reminds him.

"What do you want for your birthday, Haya?"

"I want to ride across the desert," Haya murmurs sleepily. "And go to bed with my horse beside me and my camels outside my tent. I want to be a real Arabian Princess."

Her father kisses her on the forehead. "Goodnight, Haya," he whispers as she falls asleep.

CHAPTER 5

The Foaling

Haya knew she should never have let Ali play in her room. Little brothers always stick their noses into your stuff.

"Hey, what is this?" Ali asks as he crawls out from beneath the bed with the golden shoebox grasped in his hands.

"It's nothing," Haya insists. But before she can stop him Ali has taken off the lid and has put on Mama's sunglasses.

"No!" Haya snatches the glasses back from him. "You'll break them!"

She tries to wrestle the box off him too, but Ali won't let go. "Leave it! It's private!"

"I'm just looking," Ali says as he continues to rifle through the contents. "What is this stuff anyway?"

"Treasure," Haya says.

Ali digs to the bottom of the box and holds up a photograph. It is black and white and the edges are worn from being held so often. A beautiful woman wearing the sunglasses that Ali has just tried on is smiling at the camera and holding a bright-eyed, dark-haired baby in her arms.

"Is that you or me?" Ali asks.

"It's me," Haya says quietly. "You weren't born, I don't think."

Ali looks at the picture in silence, as if he is trying to place himself in it, even though Haya has just told him he was never there.

"Are there any pictures with me too?" Ali asks.

"Not in here." Haya shakes her head.

Ali gazes at the photograph wistfully. "You had Mama for longer than me," he says.

Haya's eyes well with tears. Does that make her the lucky one, she wonders? Ali can hardly remember life when Mama was here. But Haya can, and it only makes her absence so much more awful.

"Are these real?" Ali asks, his eyes diverted like a

magpie that has spotted something sparkly. He picks up the tiny metal casings and examines them, peering inside each one. Haya complains that she wants her treasure box back, that it makes her anxious to have its contents spread out like this. What if Frances came in and found them?

"Frances is a meany," Ali confirms.

*

That afternoon, as usual, Frances has a lesson plan of mathematics and English, followed by violin, piano and dance. It hardly leaves any time to visit Amina.

Amina's belly is enormous and tight like a drum now. Each day Haya is surprised to see that the mare has grown even bigger than the day before. She is too heavily in foal to be ridden any more, but it is good to stretch her legs sometimes. After Haya has finished brushing her, she takes the mare out of her box for a walk. Sometimes Haya leads Amina down the driveway, letting the mare pause at her leisure to take a pick of the flowers at its border.

Today Haya endures her afternoon of lessons and when she arrives at the stables she finds Santi with Amina in her loose box. He is crouched down, peering beneath the mare's belly.

"Come here, Titch," Santi beckons her. "You see how the udders are swollen with milk? It means the foal is very close. It is due any day now."

"Why is she sniffing herself?" Haya asks as she watches Amina turning to snuffle at her distended belly.

"That is another sign," Santi says. "The foal will come soon, I think."

Haya sits down quietly in Amina's loose box to wait for her to have the baby. She waits and waits. It is late in the afternoon when she sticks her head round the corner of Santi's office. "Nothing is happening," Haya tells him.

"A watched pot never boils," Santi says. "I am sure her foal will come this evening."

"Can I come and help like you said I could?" Haya asks.

Santi nods. "I'll send the driver back for your things. You can stay here tonight with me and Ursula at the house and wait for the foal to come."

Frances makes a fuss of course. His Majesty is away on business and she makes it clear that she is not at all happy about this new arrangement, but eventually the driver arrives at the stables to drop off the bag and Haya makes her way up the hill to Santi's little house surrounded by a grove of olive trees.

Santi's wife Ursula is blonde and has blue eyes and laughs a lot, but not in a fake way like Happy Frances. Ursula is always in jodhpurs, even when she is not riding, and she is still dressed in them that evening as she chops the vegetables while Santi prepares the roast chicken with olives and preserved lemons. After they have eaten, Haya doesn't want to go to bed, but Ursula is firm. "You need to get some sleep so that you can be useful when the foal comes," she reasons.

"Promise to wake me," Haya insists as Ursula tucks her in.

It is almost three in the morning when Ursula comes back in and rocks Haya gently on the shoulder to rouse her.

"Haya," she whispers. "Get dressed. It has begun."

Haya is glad that she has a torch; it's really dark on the path from the house to the stables. The beam of light ahead of her wobbles as her hands shake with excitement.

Santi is already in the loose box when she arrives. He is leaning against the wall, watching Amina as she paces her stall, pawing at the straw bedding on the floor.

Eventually Amina gives a grunt and drops to her knees, lying down on her side. The mare is covered in sweat and her body is shiny and damp. She lies down for a while, raising her head from time to time to sniff her belly.

"This is it," Santi says expectantly. But Amina heaves herself to her feet and stands up again.

"What's going on?" Haya asks. "Is she OK?"

"She's fine," Santi reassures her. "Amina is getting ready. The foal will come soon."

But the foal does not come. The minutes tick by and Amina lies down and stands up again many times. She is sweating so much that a white froth has formed on her neck. Santi has beads of perspiration on his forehead as he grabs hold of Amina by the halter and urges the mare back to her feet.

He rolls his sleeves up. "Ursula," he says, "take hold of her head for me."

Ursula frowns. "You think something's wrong?"

Santi washes his hands in the soapy water bucket and then applies grease from a tub in the medicine kit along his right arm. He steps round behind Amina and lifts up the mare's tail.

"The mare is taking too long," he says. "I am going to check on the position of the foal."

Carefully, gently, Santi extends his arm to reach inside the mare, to find where the foal is. Haya stands next to Ursula and strokes Amina on her hot, wet neck, murmuring the whole time, telling the mare it is going to be OK.

When Santi withdraws his arm, his face is grim. "Ursula," he says, "go and fetch the vet. Now."

As they wait for Ursula and the vet, Haya helps to rub the mare down all over with a soft, dry towel. Amina is shivering and when Haya strokes the mare's face she can see the whites of her eyes. "Don't be afraid," she whispers. "The vet will be here soon." It has only been a few minutes since Ursula left, but it feels like forever. When the mare tries to lie down again, Santi asks Haya if she is strong enough to hold the halter while he moves around the mare and pushes her to keep her upright.

"I think Amina's foal is breech," Santi explains. "Foals are supposed to come out front first, but this one's head is in the wrong place. We need the vet to come and help get the foal out."

There is nothing more they can do but wait. Haya holds Amina's head in her arms. The mare is trembling and Haya whispers to her. "Not much longer, Amina. He's coming, I promise."

The lights come on in the courtyard as Ursula returns with the vet. Amina is drenched with sweat, shivering and exhausted. She does not even turn her head to look when the vet greases his arm and begins to search inside for the foal.

"It's a breech," he confirms. "I'll try to turn it."

Santi nods and takes the mare's head as the vet moves back to the tail once more.

Haya stands beside Amina's shoulder and watches the vet as he works. He is taking forever and all the time Amina looks weaker and more miserable. "Don't be scared," Haya murmurs. But now she is afraid for Amina. The vet is taking too long.

Finally the vet pulls his arm back out and shakes his head. "I'm sorry," he says, "the foal can't be turned."

He says nothing more, but that is enough. Santi understands what must happen next.

"Ursula," Santi says, "please take Titch back home to Al Nadwa."

Haya is bewildered. Amina's foal is still stuck! The mare needs help and suddenly Santi is sending her away?

"Please, no," Haya says. "I want to see the foal being born. I won't get in the way, I promise. I'll stay back in the corner of the box, I can help…"

Next to Amina the vet begins to unpack the contents of his bag. The syringes, scalpels and instruments are laid out in a row on a dark green cloth spread out on the straw.

"What is he doing?"

"He is going to save the mare if he can," Santi says. He cannot meet Haya's eyes. "Ursula, take the Princess home."

*

As they pull up to the entrance of the palace, Haya emerges from the car trembling and exhausted. Her clothes are caked with dust and horse sweat and her cheeks are stained with tears. If only Mama were here to take her in her arms and hold her tight and never let go. But at the top of the stairs, waiting with arms folded, is Frances.

"Oh, Haya..." There is something about the look that Frances gives her that makes Haya's eyes brim with tears all over again. She wants comfort so desperately. She swallows her pride and runs up the stairs towards the governess.

Frances shakes her head. "Look at the state of you! Your boots are covered in mud. And your fingernails! My heavens, child, you are utterly filthy and you positively reek—"

That is it. Haya doesn't listen to any more. She pushes

past Frances, choking on her tears, and runs in muddy boots past the row of Kings, bounding upstairs. The slam of her bedroom door echoes throughout the palace.

In the darkness, Haya drops to the floor and drags herself beneath the bed until she reaches her treasure box. She shimmies back out again with the box and lies panting on the floor. Her hands are shaking so much that she cannot open the lid. Instead, she just clutches it to her chest, holding it close to her heart as she shudders and cries, her sobs wracking her body as she weeps and weeps until she has no more tears.

Chapter 6

The Birthday Present

Haya opens her eyes. It is morning and the sun is shining through her bedroom window, but it is not the sun that has woken her. It is the sound of the voices downstairs at the front door. Slipping out of bed, she runs across the landing into Ali's room. He is already at the bedroom window, peering out at the commotion below.

"Ursula is here," he says with his nose pressed up to the glass. "Her and Frances are fighting."

Haya looks out of the window. She can see Ursula standing on the doorstep, still wearing the same clothes that she had on when she dropped Haya home the night before. And standing in front of her, hands on hips, flanked by the stone lions, is Frances.

"This is ridiculous," Ursula says. "Let me in. I need to see Haya."

"Out of the question," Frances replies. "The Princess is still in bed. She's exhausted after last night. She is not fit to receive company."

"Well, I'll come back later then."

"I'd prefer it if you didn't," Frances says.

"It's not up to you," Ursula snaps back. "Ask Haya! She needs to know what happened."

Frances looks as stony-faced as the lions. "I'm not asking a five-year-old to make the decisions; I'm the one who is in charge. If it had been up to me, she would never have been there in the first place. She was in floods of tears last night when you brought her home."

"But I should tell her—"

"No," Frances says. "You have already done enough damage without upsetting the Princess all over again. Now I think it's time you got back in your car and left before I call the guards."

Haya leaps down off the window seat and begins to run. Across the landing and down the stairs, she feels her heart hammering in her chest as she races for the front door. Why does the palace have to be so big? She is halfway down the corridor when she sees Frances striding towards her.

"Where is she?" Haya pants.

"If you mean Ursula, she has gone," Frances replies. "Now go upstairs, Haya, and get dressed for breakfast."

Haya is beside herself. "But I wanted to see her..."

"Out of the question."

"I want to know what happened to Amina..."

"Haya, do not argue with me," Frances says. "That is all."

*

What else can Haya do? It is another two whole days before Baba returns from his meeting in America and Frances won't let Haya go back to the stables no matter how much she begs.

When the King arrives home, it is late at night. Haya is in bed, but still awake when he comes in to check on her. "You're back," she murmurs.

"I made it just in time," her father says as he strokes her hair. "I know a girl who is turning six tomorrow."

*

The birthday party is held on the lawn of the palace. All of Haya's cousins, aunts and uncles are there. Her aunts all admire the pretty dress that Frances made her wear. They say to Haya: "You look so much like your mother," and Haya feels her cheeks turn hot with pride and delight.

She misses Mama more than ever on her birthday. Special days should be happy occasions, but since Mama died there is a tinge of sadness about them. But you cannot stop birthdays; they come every year. And so Haya tries to be brave and to smile for the guests even though she hears her aunts as they whisper, *How quiet she is! And how sad she looks. Look how she sits alone and doesn't play with the other children. It is no wonder that the King constantly worries about her.*

"Haya," her father says, "come over here and play pin the tail on the donkey."

Haya's father puts a blindfold on her and spins her round and round until she thinks she is going to topple over. All the other children shriek and giggle as she tries to stick the tail on the donkey's head and soon Haya is smiling too.

Lunch is a picnic on the lawn and there is birthday cake and Haya opens the presents stacked on a big table. The coloured paper crackles in her fingers as she thanks her aunts and uncles for the gifts.

"My present wouldn't fit on the table," her father says. "It's waiting at the front door."

The children run, screaming with excitement, as

they race through the palace, their bare feet slapping on marble. Haya is in the lead ahead of Ali and her cousins, determined to be the first one there. The massive front doors of Al Nadwa have already been swung open wide and she races outside.

"What is it?" Ali is panting. "What did he get you…?"

Haya does not answer. She is too shocked by the sight that greets her. At the bottom of the stairs, seated upon camels, are two officers of the Desert Patrol, the most rugged and fearless soldiers in all of Arabia.

The men of the Desert Patrol carry curved daggers at their hips. Their faces are noble, tanned from the sun, with high chiselled cheekbones and black eyes, their expressions solemn and serious. If the stone lions at the palace doors of Al Nadwa could shrink back in awe of these men, they would!

"Do you like them?" Her father has caught up with her at last.

Haya looks at him, her eyes wide. Standing next to these officers with enormous pink bows tied round their necks are her presents. Two camels. One fully grown, the other just a baby, but still taller than Haya. The baby camel keeps shaking his head to get rid of the pink ribbon, as if it is embarrassing him.

"They are mine? Both of them?" Haya turns to look at her father in astonishment.

"You wanted to be a proper Arabian Princess," the King smiles. "For this you will need camels."

Baba has understood all along. *A proper Arabian Princess* is exactly what she wants to be.

"Will they live with us at the palace?"

Haya can feel her governess's cold eyes boring into her. She knows Frances is imagining the mess Haya's camels will make on the back lawn!

Luckily for Frances, the King doesn't think this is a good idea either. "They will remain with the Desert Patrol," he said. "But you may visit them to feed and ride them."

Haya is hesitant as she steps close to the camels. "Can I pat the little one?"

"Of course, Your Royal Highness," the soldier replies.

Haya reaches out a hand to stroke the baby camel. He has shaggy fur, soft like velvet, the colour of caramel.

"I'm going to call this one Fluffy," she says decisively, "and the mummy can be Lulabelle."

A choked noise comes from the officer holding Fluffy's lead rope. The men of the Desert Patrol are the toughest soldiers in Arabia. They do not call their camels

Fluffy and Lulabelle! But he keeps a straight face and says nothing. He waits patiently while Haya and Ali and their cousins fuss over the baby and the other officer gets down off his camel to lift up the children so they can take turns to sit on Lulabelle's back. When at last everyone has had enough, the soldiers mount up once more and lead the camels away, both men looking exhausted. The perils of the great desert are nothing compared to a six-year-old's birthday party!

On the steps of the palace, guests are preparing to leave when Santi and Ursula arrive. They are driving the Al Hummar truck, and Ursula waves cheerily out of the window. "Happy birthday, Haya!" she calls. "So sorry we're late!"

"Yes, happy birthday, Titch," Santi says warmly.

"You've missed the birthday cake, I'm afraid," Frances says curtly.

Santi pulls the truck up and opens the door, patting his belly as he gets out. "I do not need cake. Ursula feeds me too well as it is."

He smiles at Haya. "I am only here to bring Titch her present."

Santi looks over at the King and Haya sees her father give him a nod, as if to confirm that all is fine.

"There is another gift," her father says, bending down beside Haya. "Santi and Ursula have brought it here for you."

Haya does not know why her heart is beating so fast. Her father takes her by the hand and leads her to the rear of the truck, where Ursula and Santi undo the bolts and lower the ramp.

Inside the truck, so small that it does not even take up the space of one horse stall, is her birthday present. It looks at Haya with wide eyes blinking in the sunlight, a bundle of fuzzy baby fur on lanky pipe-cleaner legs.

"It's a horse!" Ali shouts out. Then he frowns. "Why is it so little?"

"It's a foal," Haya tells him. "A baby, Ali, like you."

"I'm not a baby. I'm four," Ali says indignantly. But Haya isn't listening to her brother. All her focus is on the foal standing before her.

It is a bay, with four black stocking legs and a thick black bottlebrush mane that sticks up in a ruffle along its tiny neck. On its forehead there is a white star and on one of the hind legs there is a white sock with black ermine dots on it.

With a stocky little body and sturdy limbs, the foal is no elegant, long-stemmed beauty like the rose-grey horses of Al Hummar. Yet its heavy jaw and flat profile are handsome in their own way. And those eyes! The foal has the most amazing eyes, so big and brown and wide, honest and kind. Haya looks into them and her heart beats faster still. She has never seen a horse quite so beautiful in her entire life.

Haya has been staring so long at the foal, she has forgotten the guests. When at last she turns back to them, her mouth is wide open, but no words come out and the crowd laughs.

"Is it mine?" she manages to stammer.

"She is yours," her father says.

She. That was what her father just said. So the foal is a filly. A baby girl.

The King leads Haya by the hand up the ramp. When they get close to the filly, Haya can see that she is shivering.

"She's cold," Haya says.

"She's just a little scared," the King says.

"Why?" Haya asks.

"She's never left her loose box before," the King says, looking at his daughter kindly. "The world can be a frightening place when you are very little and all alone."

The King crouches down beside his daughter and puts

his arm round her. "This filly is Amina's baby, Haya. The vet could not save the mare, but he did everything he could so that her foal might live."

Now Haya knows what Ursula came to tell her when Frances sent her away. This shivering bundle of fluff is Amina's daughter. She is three days old and she is an orphan.

"She will need a great deal of care," Baba is saying. "It is a big responsibility."

Haya looks at the foal. Now she can see how much like her mother this filly is. Her coat is still fluff, but already it is a rich red bay, just like her mama. And her eyes, they are Amina's eyes: deep liquid brown, gentle and kind.

"What do I have to do?" Haya asks shakily.

"Feed her, groom her, teach her manners. Teach her how to become a horse," her father says. "Santi and the grooms will help you, but she is your foal, Haya. You will be her mother now."

Haya feels the weight of his words. This foal that clung on so tenaciously to life, and remains in this world against the odds, is now being given over to her care.

Haya reaches out a hand and strokes the trembling filly. "It's OK," she says softly. "Don't be afraid, little one. No one is going to hurt you."

The party guests are crowding the truck, trying to get a better look. "If everyone moves back then Ursula can lead her out," the King says.

The party guests retreat to the steps as Haya and the King come down the ramp first and then Ursula comes after them leading the foal. Gently, step by step, she coaxes the filly forward until she comes down all in a rush, legs wobbling down the ramp as if she is attempting to walk it on stilts.

When she reaches the bottom, the filly stops at the sight of the party guests. Her ears prick forward and she takes deep, snorty breaths through wide nostrils. Then she raises her head as high as she can and lets out a valiant whinny. It is meant to be a clarion call, but instead it comes out as a shrill squeak. The crowd laughs and the foal is startled by the loud noise. She skitters back and gives another snort, body trembling and eyes wide.

"Do you want to hold her?" Ursula passes Haya the lead rope. Haya takes it and stand at arm's length, still unable to believe that this creature belongs to her. She looks up at her father, her eyes shining.

"Thank you, Baba," she says solemnly. "I love her. She is so beautiful."

"Are you going to ride her now?" Ali asks.

Haya turns to her brother. "No!"

"Can I ride her then?" Ali asks.

"Ali," the King says, "she is just a foal. You can't ride her until she is grown up."

"You have to break her in first," Haya says. This is something she has heard Santi say about the rose-grey fillies.

"Well, how long will that be?" Ali frowns.

"In three years she should be ready," the King tells him.

Ali sighs. "I want a bike for my birthday. You can ride a bike straight away."

The laughter of the party guests makes the foal skitter again.

"I think that's enough excitement for one day maybe?" Santi says to Haya. "She is ready to go home. It is almost her dinnertime."

"What does she eat?" Haya asks.

"Camel's milk," Santi says. "I will show you how to give her the bottle. You must feed her four times a day – and three times during the night too."

There is a loud harrumph from among the crowd and then Happy Frances, her voice coated in honey, speaks up.

"Señor Lopez," Happy Frances says, "surely you are not suggesting that Her Royal Highness will be at your stables at all hours of the night feeding this waif?"

Santi shrugs. "The foal belongs to Haya. It is her responsibility," he says. "That is all I am saying."

Frances turns and makes her appeal to the King. "But Señor Lopez must see it is not reasonable for the Princess to be travelling at such an hour? Let the stablehands do the feeding."

"I have to do it," Haya insists. "She's mine. I'm the one who is taking care of her."

"Out of the question." Frances refuses to give in. "It is too far, in the dark on those roads..."

"Frances is right," the King says. And Haya thinks for an awful moment he is taking the governess's side, but then the King turns to the crowd. "My brother?" he says. "Can we keep the filly at your stables instead?"

Prince Hassan is the King's brother and captain of the Royal Polo Team. His polo stables are inside the Royal Compound, only a few minutes' walk up the hill from the palace.

"Certainly," Prince Hassan agrees. "There are plenty of spare loose boxes. My polo mares will enjoy the company."

Haya's uncle sends word to his grooms at the polo yards to prepare a box for their new addition, and Ursula leads the filly back into the truck.

"Do you want to ride with her?" she asks Haya.

Nervously, Haya climbs the ramp of the horse truck. Her eyes are as wide as those of the filly beside her. "You'll be OK," Ursula insists. "All you need to do is hold her halter like this, and talk to her once we start to move to keep her calm."

Ursula smiles and then steps out of the truck and raises the ramp behind her. Haya can hear the locks slide on the outside of the doors.

"Hang on to the rail when we move off!" she hears Ursula shout. "It might be a bit bumpy at first."

It is dark inside with the door shut, but two thin windows along the side walls provide enough daylight to see by. Haya uses one hand to steady herself on the railings, gripping the foal's halter with the other hand.

Haya and the foal are alone together for the first time. Haya stares at the bay filly as if it were some magical creature, as if she had been given a unicorn.

"Hello," she says to the filly. "I knew you before you were born. You look just like your mama, do you know that? She was very beautiful, and she was a great jumper.

And you are just like her."

She strokes the filly down her broad muzzle, pressing her face close to it in the darkness. Now she is whispering, "My name is Haya and I'm going to look after you."

She holds tight to the filly's halter and her father's words fill the silence between them. *You will be her mother now.*

"I'm going to take care of you," Haya whispers. "You will never be lonely or sad because I will love you always. I will be there no matter what happens and you will make your mama proud and be the best horse in Arabia."

In the back of the horse truck, the bay filly nickers softly, and Haya knows that she understands every word.

CHAPTER 7

Bint Al-Reeh

Prince Hassan's polo mares crane their heads over the loose-box doors at the stables, whinnying and nickering their greetings to the newcomer.

Frightened by their attentions, the filly clings so close to Haya down the ramp, she almost tramples her. She stands in the yard, wide-eyed and trembling, as she takes in the sights and sounds.

The polo mares are Thoroughbreds with muscular necks and Roman noses. They wear their manes hogged down to a stump, the hair shaved away along the crest so that the reins don't get tangled in the heat of a match.

This is a working yard. Unlike Al Hummar, there are no magnificent grey-green olive trees or elegant fountains. The horses drink from battered plastic water troughs and stretch their legs in dusty pens.

The stable block itself is modern and elegant with high walls like a fortress, the two dozen loose boxes arranged in a U-shape round a large central concrete courtyard for tacking up and washing down.

Haya takes in the scent of manure and horse sweat and her heart immediately leaps, just as it does at Al Hummar. "Come on." She leads the filly forward. "Let's see your new home."

The filly skips alongside her. By the time they reach the loose box her coat is damp with sweat. When Haya unclips her lead rope and lets her loose inside the box, the filly rushes straight to the stable door, her tiny muzzle raised up in a desperate attempt to see over the top, her plaintive whinnies echoing through the stables.

"She doesn't like it," Haya says. "Maybe she wants to go back to Al Hummar."

Santi shakes his head. "It is not her home that she calls out for, it is her mother."

The filly gives another desperate whinny, her tiny nostrils trembling, and Haya is suddenly in the kitchen at the Summer House, an armful of oranges tumbling to the floor. *Poor foal. She thinks that if she cries loud enough her mother will come back for her.*

"The filly will settle down soon," Prince Hassan reassures them. "My grooms will make sure she is well fed."

Haya is tired and hungry. The last thing she ate was a slice of birthday cake at midday and now the sun is getting low in the sky. Right now she would dearly love to return to Al Nadwa. There are birthday gifts waiting for her. But the filly calls and calls for her mama. Haya turns to her uncle.

"I must stay," Haya quietly insists. "I have to. She needs me."

*

It is one thing to be selfless and noble in the daylight, but in the darkness it is a different matter. Santi and Ursula have left to give the horses at Al Hummar their evening feeds. Prince Hassan has gone home and the grooms at the polo stables have finished work until tomorrow. It is just Haya in the yard with her bodyguards outside the stable gates.

After much fretting, the filly has finally exhausted herself and fallen asleep. She lies on the straw bedding in the corner. Haya nestles into the straw on the floor beside her. She wishes she had thought to ask for a blanket. The summer nights are getting colder and there is a bite to the air even inside the loose box. Also, for the past hour, she has been trying very hard to ignore the strange noises coming from the yard outside. She can hear something scratching, but whenever she sticks her head out of the stall, the noise goes quiet. It is probably just the stable cat on the hunt for mice, she tells herself. She clambers up out of the straw to peer over the stable door. It's very dark, far too dark to see anything. She sits down, with her back against the loose-box wall. *It's OK, nothing's there. Just the cat.*

A moment later, the security lights flicker on and Haya gasps as she hears footsteps coming across the courtyard, getting closer. An intruder! She must protect her foal.

"Haya!"

Two eyes are peering at her from over the top of the stable door. It is only Ali!

"Baba said I could come to see the foal again," Ali says. "We brought you dinner."

Her father appears at the door. "Ismail has prepared you a birthday feast," he says. "Where would you like to eat?"

The tack room seems like the best place. The King finds a wooden bench from the stable yard so they place the food on it and sit on the wooden saddle horses. It feels like they are riding and eating at the same time! Ismail has packed the food into covered serving platters so it has stayed hot. There is nutty and delicious orange-scented chicken and a big platter of rice with sweet apricots.

"So what do you think of Haya's foal?" the King asks his son.

"She doesn't do much, does she?" Ali says.

"She's asleep," Haya points out.

Ali gnaws a piece of chicken, trying to make his saddle horse trot as he chews.

For dessert that night there is *barazek* – sweet honey sesame cookies that crumble as they bite into them and a flask of hot, tangy lemon drink. They go back to the loose box to see that the foal has woken up and is on her feet, sniffing at the straw and exploring her new home.

"What's her name?" Ali asks.

Haya looks at the filly, trying to negotiate her way around on gangly limbs. One day those same legs will carry her at a gallop as they race across the desert sands.

"I am going to call her Bint Al-Reeh," Haya tells her brother.

Ali giggles.

Haya frowns at him. "What's so funny?"

"Bint Al-Reeh-*a*," Ali says with a mischievous look in his eye. "Bint Al-Reeh-*a*!"

Haya glares at her brother. *Bint Al-Reeh* is Arabic. It means Daughter of the Wind. But *Bint Al-Reeh-a*, the way her brother is pronouncing it, means Daughter of the Farts.

"Stop it, Ali!" Haya wails.

But it is no use. Ali has decided that this joke is the funniest thing he has ever heard. He keeps singing "Bint Al-Reeh-a" over and over again. Eventually the King has no choice but to put him back into the car with the doors shut so that Haya can't hear him.

"Why don't you come home too now, Haya?" her father says. "One of Hassan's grooms can take over tonight, then you can come back and check on Bint Al-Reeh first thing in the morning."

Haya is wearing the warm jersey that her father brought for her, but even so she feels the cold nip of the night air. She thinks about her warm bed back at the palace. She shakes her head.

"Bint Al-Reeh knows me now. She won't miss her mother so much if I stay with her."

The King does not dispute her decision. "You must

do what you think is best." He hugs his daughter close, kisses her on the top of her head. "I like the name you have chosen for her," he says. "It is a name worthy of a great horse."

"Bint Al-Reeh is going to be a great horse," Haya says. "One day she will be the best horse in the Royal Stables."

*

After the King and Prince Ali have gone, Haya sits down on the fold-out camp bed with her sleeping bag, and pours warm camel's milk from a Thermos flask into the foal's bottle. She rests the flask on the lip of the bottle to keep it steady as she pours. Then she replaces the teat, screwing it on tight. It is time for a feed.

"Come on, Bint Al-Reeh." She grasps the filly firmly by her halter and tries to give her the teat. When Santi did it, he held the bottle right up to the filly's mouth and forced the teat in, pushing until she started to suckle.

Haya tries, but the foal is too strong for her to hold and manage the bottle at the same time and keeps pulling away. She tries manoeuvring Bint Al-Reeh into the corner of the stall, taking the halter in one hand while she tries to force the teat into the side of her muzzle. But the foal refuses to open her mouth. Her jaws are clamped shut.

"You have to drink!" Haya is almost in tears. "Please!"

She takes hold of the halter, but the filly squirms and pulls against her grip, fighting until Haya lets go and falls back exhausted on the straw. She cannot do this alone; it is impossible!

Tears of frustration are welling in Haya's eyes. If the foal doesn't feed during the night then she will grow weak and dehydrated – she might even die!

Do not think like that, she tells herself. *This is your foal, Haya. You must do this.*

She picks up the bottle again, and as she grasps it this time, a trickle of milk escapes the teat and runs down her forearm. It feels warm and sticky. Haya looks at the milk dribbling down and, without thinking, she licks it off, tasting the creamy sweetness on her tongue.

With renewed determination, she takes the foal by the halter again. This time she doesn't offer the bottle. Instead, she dribbles a few drops of camel's milk on to her thumb and then, gingerly, she holds her thumb to the foal's muzzle.

The foal sniffs her hand, ears pricked forward.

"Taste it," Haya says. "You like milk, don't you?"

The filly's tongue darts out. It is rough like warm, wet sandpaper against Haya's skin. She dribbles some more milk on to her thumb and holds it to the foal's muzzle and this time, as the filly's tongue comes out, Haya eases her thumb inside its mouth. It is the strangest sensation and it is all Haya can do not to panic that the foal might bite it. But the foal doesn't nip her. Instead, she begins to suckle. Her sucks grow stronger and more urgent, and Haya slides the teat in, withdrawing her thumb carefully so that the foal doesn't notice the exchange.

Suddenly the foal's tail begins to spin like a little furry catherine wheel. The milk begins to disappear rapidly from the bottle.

"Good girl, Bint Al-Reeh!" Haya almost cries with relief. She holds the bottle with both hands as the sucks grow even more vigorous as the bottle empties. "Good girl."

Two more times during the night Haya wakes up to feed her foal. Each time she uses the same trick and by morning, when her father returns, he finds the Thermos of milk empty at the door and Haya fast asleep, curled up in the straw, with her filly beside her.

Chapter 8

The Desert Patrol

Haya does not leave Bint Al-Reeh's side. She eats her meals in the loose box and at night she sleeps on the cot with Bint Al-Reeh next to her in the straw.

Each morning, at Frances's insistence, she comes home to shower, get dressed and eat breakfast before promptly going back to the stables.

"It is only the child's health I am concerned about," Haya overhears Happy Frances telling Baba. "She cannot possibly continue like this; she is pale and exhausted."

"She is smiling," the King says, "and laughing and talking. For the first time since her mother died, there is a light in her eyes again."

"The foal is taking up so much of her time." Happy

Frances tries a different tack. "A growing girl needs fresh air and the company of other children. And what about her studies? She has not done anything all week other than tend to the foal."

"Some lessons are more important than school," replies the King. "And our best teachers have four legs."

*

"Are you going back to the stables *again*?" Ali asks as he watches his sister packing her bag. "I don't see what's so special about that foal anyway. Most of the time she just sleeps."

Haya smiles. Men and boys never seem to find the endless things to do in the stables that she does. Ali and her uncle come to ride, and care for their horses, feed and treat them well, but Haya is happy just to *be* there.

Ali has a football tucked under his arm. "Stay here and play with me," he offers. "We can have kicks in the garden."

Haya shakes her head. "I can't, Ali. It is almost time to feed her."

Ali mutters something about horses being boring and stomps off. Haya feels bad. She knows her brother misses her company, but the filly needs her too. It is impossible to explain to Ali how she feels when she is with her foal.

It is as if they are two halves of the same heart and one half cannot beat without the other.

"Bint Al-Reeh-a!" Ali sticks his head back round the bedroom door. "Daughter of the Farts!"

"She is called Bree," Haya tells him firmly. It is the filly's new nickname, short for Bint Al-Reeh.

"Bint Al-Reeh-a," Ali chants again, delighting in being able to annoy his sister with the addition of just one letter.

Haya sighs in defeat and leaves for the stables once more.

At Prince Hassan's yards, Bree is always waiting, with her tiny muzzle barely visible, nostrils twitching over the stable door.

When Haya enters the loose box, the filly nickers happily, nuzzling up against her, pushing Haya with her muzzle, searching for milk. There is no need for Haya to do her thumb trick any more. Bree takes the teat as soon as it is offered and drinks with gusto, her tiny tail twirling a vigorous circle as she suckles.

Haya watches the camel's milk disappearing from the bottle in her hand and feels satisfied as she thinks about it filling up Bree's belly.

Bree keeps drinking, even when the bottle is

completely empty, suckling optimistically for a while longer. Then she pricks her ears forward and gets a wild look about her, her nostrils widening. Haya has seen this look before – the filly is in one of her playful moods. Haya has just enough time to get out of the way before Bree surges forward, putting on a sudden burst of speed, and begins tearing madly about the loose box, circling Haya at a chaotic canter, her long legs plunging into the thick straw bedding of her stall with each stride.

After a few laps, she stops and raises her head to give a shrill-pitched whinny, then she goes up on her hindquarters like a stallion, her front legs striking out, lashing at an imaginary foe.

Haya giggles at her. Bree snorts indignantly and does one more mad lap of the loose box before finally pulling up to a halt and collapsing back down into the straw. In just a few moments, she is fast asleep.

The polo mares recognise Haya now when she comes to the yard. They nicker cheerful greetings in the hope that she will feed them. Sometimes she helps Hassan's grooms mix their morning feeds, slopping the boiled barley in with the alfalfa chaff.

"Would you like a job here, Your Royal Highness?" the head groom asks Haya. "I could do with an extra pair of hands and you are always here bright and early."

Santi comes to check on Bree most days and one afternoon he arrives at the stables with the horse float behind his car. "Come and see, Titch!"

The mare that he unloads from the trailer is old and her grey dapples have faded so that she is quite white. Her legs and neck are skinny, but her belly looks huge and sticks out at the sides.

"Is she for me?" Haya asks.

"No," Santi says. "She is for the foal. I drove all the way to Wadi Rum to get her. Her name is Latifah. She can be a nurse mare for Bree."

Santi strokes the mare's neck. "She had her own baby, but it died. You see how her udders are swollen still with the milk? She can be a mother for the filly."

"But I can feed Bree," Haya says defensively. "I can care for her all by myself."

Santi sees the hurt look in the girl's eyes.

"Titch, I know that you have been working very, very hard," he says. "If you had not cared for Bree with such devotion these past days then the filly would not have lived. She has grown to depend on you. Perhaps she even thinks of you as her mother now. And this is a wonderful thing," Santi hesitates, "...but it can also be risky. A foal learns manners from its mother, and an orphan like Bree can become bossy and aggressive."

"But I'm teaching her good manners," Haya insists. "She picks up her hooves for me and lets me brush her."

"Haya," Santi says, "you are doing a very good job, but some things only a mare can teach a foal. What will you do if Bree decides to lash out at you with her hind legs because she demands more milk? A mare would bite her and kick her straight back, put her in her place. This filly is growing up fast. One day very soon she will be bigger than you and the little habits that you thought were so cute will become dangerous."

She doesn't want to admit it, but Santi is right. Already Haya can feel the filly shoving so hard against the bottle when she feeds her that Haya finds it difficult to hold on. And the filly is barely a week old! Imagine when she has grown stronger, how tough it will be to feed her then. If Haya is the mother, like her father said, then she must do what is best for Bree.

"OK," she agrees reluctantly.

Haya expects Santi to put Latifah in the same box as Bree, but he leads the mare into the loose box next door to the foal. "We do this slowly," he tells Haya. "That way there is less risk the mare will attack."

Attack? Santi did not mention this before!

Haya watches anxiously as Latifah approaches the small window with steel bars that connects the two loose boxes. The mare can smell the foal and she thrusts her slender muzzle up to the bars, her nostrils flared wide, her breath coming hard in short, inquisitive snorts.

On the other side of the wall, Bree is intrigued. She comes close enough to look through the hole and then, without actually moving her legs, she stretches her neck, extending her muzzle closer to Latifah. She gives the mare a sniff and then suddenly her tail starts swishing madly back and forth with delight. Bree starts to nicker vigorously to Latifah, imploring the mare to come to her and Haya feels her stomach make a hard knot. How heartbroken the foal will be if the mare rejects her!

"Santi." Haya's voice is anxious. "What if Latifah doesn't want her?"

Latifah takes a step towards the foal and when their muzzles connect the mare takes a deep snort. Suddenly her ears flatten back in anger as she lets out a vicious squeal, lashing out at the filly with a swift blow of her foreleg!

"Bree!" Haya panics and tries to open the loose-box door to get to her, but Santi stops her. "She's OK. The mare cannot hurt her through the wall."

Haya isn't so sure, but she does as Santi says and waits and watches, scarcely daring to breathe as Latifah steps forward again to sniff at the foal through the gap in the wall. Miraculously, the mare seems to have a change of heart. Her ears prick forward and she begins to nicker affectionately, nuzzling at the foal through the bars.

"She likes her!" Haya is almost in tears with relief.

Santi does not rush things. He lets the mare and foal continue their greeting ritual through the bars for what seems like forever, before he grunts his satisfaction and moves Latifah at last into Bree's stall.

The mare and foal sniff each other all over and then there is a tense moment when the filly puts her head beneath the mare's belly for the first time, searching for the udder. Haya worries that the mare might turn nasty again. But Latifah stands perfectly still as Bree latches on to feed. Her tail begins to whirl as the milk flows.

Santi looks at Haya and is surprised when he sees the tears rolling down her cheeks. "What's wrong, Titch?"

Haya wipes the tears away roughly, shaking her head, not wanting to embarrass herself further.

"What is it?" Santi insists.

"She doesn't need me any more. She has a new

mother now."

Santi laughs. "Haya, she has a nurse mare to give her milk, but she will need you more than ever as she grows up. Who else will teach her how to stand still and be groomed, or how to be loaded on to a horse trailer, eat from a feed bin or wear a saddle and bridle and carry a rider? This filly has much to learn and you must be the one to teach her."

He smiles at the sight of the mare and the foal feeding. "You haven't been replaced. You just have a little help, that is all."

That night Latifah stays in the loose box with Bree and, for the first time in almost a week, Haya sleeps in her bed at Al Nadwa. The mattress feels so soft and her bedroom smells of sweet orange blossom and, despite the fact that Frances makes her do maths homework and practise the violin for a whole hour before dinner, she is glad to be home.

*

Now there are more new rules set by Frances. According to the governess, it is not appropriate for children to have the run of the house and suddenly, for no reason at all, Baba's office is out of bounds.

"Your father needs privacy to work," Frances says.

"A King's office is full of important papers, it is not a playground."

But Frances cannot keep watch all the time and, in the mornings, when the governess is out of sight, Haya and Ali sneak inside and tiptoe across the bearskin rug. Underneath the desk, where Frances cannot see, there is a secret place where they leave notes for Baba. Sometimes he leaves notes back for them too. They are like secret agents passing messages and Frances is the enemy.

Today the secret note that has been written for Baba is scrawled in pink felt-tip and it says just three words: 'Haya loves Baba.'

Haya carries the note tucked up her sleeve as she pads barefooted along the corridor. Outside her father's office she stops and waits, listening for footsteps, then she casts a furtive glance towards the kitchen. There is no one coming. She reaches out and grasps the door handle and then steps inside the office and shuts the door behind her.

The office is gloomy and still. Dust motes can be seen floating in the shafts of morning light that penetrate the windows along the east wall.

Haya feels the bearskin prickling the bare soles of her feet as she moves silently across the office, heading for her Baba's desk. She has put the note in the secret place and she is about to leave when she sees the statue. It is on a pedestal next to the window. It is a falcon, life-sized and cast from bronze. It is so sleek and powerful, the bronze feathers glinting in the sunlight, noble head held aloft with an imperious expression.

Haya walks towards the statue to take a closer look. She is just a few metres away when she reaches out a hand to touch it and then freezes. The statue just blinked at her.

The bird is alive! Cruel eyes, the colour of amber, are now trained on her as if she were prey.

Slowly Haya begins to back away. As she does this, the great bird fixes her with his gaze, cocks his head to one side, contemplating his next move. Haya can feel her heart pounding. Will he attack her if she tries to run? She steps backwards ever so slowly, and has almost reached the door when it swings open and her father enters the room.

"Baba!" She is so scared she forgets that she shouldn't even be in her father's office. "Your new statue is going to eat me!"

The King laughs. "I see you have met Akhbar," he says. At the sound of his voice the falcon suddenly animates himself with a vigorous shake of his feathers and gives a shriek.

The King walks across the office towards the falcon, and crooks his elbow, like a man putting out his arm to ask a lady to waltz. "Akhbar!"

With a single, elegant flap, Akhbar gracefully dismounts his perch and leaps on to the King's forearm. Haya watches her father stroke the bird, his fingers tracing a line between the bird's fierce amber eyes.

"Akhbar will be coming with us today."

*

They travel by jeep that morning, a motorcade of four military vehicles with roll bars, but no roofs, painted in army camouflage colours. In the first jeep three soldiers of the King's Guard travel in military uniform. In the second jeep the King travels in the front seat beside his driver. Akhbar rides upfront too, perched on the King's shoulder. The falcon's legs are tethered by long leather straps and he wears a tiny leather hood over his head so that his eyes are hidden and only his razor-sharp beak remains poking out.

Haya sits in the back seat with Ali. He has wrapped his keffiyeh completely round his face just like the soldiers do, so that only his eyes peek out, squinting in the glare of the desert sun. Haya wishes that she had one to mask her face because the dust flies up in a cloud around them as they travel, coating everything in fine, gritty sand.

There is a fifth passenger in the car with them, a sleek saluki, a pure-bred hunting dog, built for speed, like a greyhound except bigger, with a silken coat of long silver hair. All the way on their long journey, the saluki sits there with his muzzle quivering as he sniffs at the air. Haya worries that the dog might try to bite Akhbar, but the saluki seems utterly disinterested in the falcon as he stares out at the desert horizon.

They are not driving on roads today, but following the rutted, worn tracks used by Bedouin nomads. At times, the sand turns soft beneath them, almost like quicksand, so deep that the wheels of the jeep sink and flounder. At other times, the terrain is so rutted and rocky Haya has to keep both hands holding tight to stop herself being flung into the air.

Deeper and deeper into the desert they travel, and then on the horizon Haya spies something big and black rising up out of the sand.

It is a Bedouin tent. As the jeeps get closer to the camp, Haya can see the wide-open tent mouth and the men of the Desert Patrol coming out to meet them. Their Chief Officer is a handsome man with high cheekbones and she recognises him as Major Jafar, the same man who brought the camels Lulabelle and Fluffy to the palace on her birthday.

"Your Majesty." Major Jafar gives a reverential bow to the King. "I hope your journey has not been too unpleasant." He gestures to the patrol's camels tethered beside the tent, dressed in their colourful Bedouin saddles strung with tassels. "In the desert, the camel is best transport."

While Major Jafar's men make preparations for their onward journey, he welcomes the royal party inside where strong black tea is served, piping hot and still tasting of the embers of the fire, with lots of sugar to make it very sweet. Haya and Ali sit cross-legged on cushions sipping their tea while the King talks with Major Jafar. Haya notices how happy her Baba seems here with his men and she realises that, to her father, the desert is truly home.

One of the Bedouin, a desert soldier in uniform like the rest with a curved dagger at his hip and a gun slung across his back, has been watching as Haya and Ali finish their second cup of tea and now he approaches Haya.

"You want to see your camels?" he asks. His voice is gruff, but his eyes are very kind. She nods.

"Come with me."

The camels are tethered on long ropes in a row in the sand. Their legs are hobbled with leather straps and they have saddles on their backs with the girths loosened off so that they can rest comfortably. They stare for a moment at Haya and Ali, then continue to munch at the chaff in the feedbags strapped to their faces.

Lulabelle is the fourth camel in the line. Fluffy is curled up alongside her and is now old enough to have a feedbag of his own too. On the baby camel, however, the feedbag almost swamps his entire face and all you can see of him is a pair of wide brown eyes and long fluttering lashes.

"They remember, eh, Haya?" the Bedouin says. "They know they belong to you." He beckons her closer. "Here, you can stroke them. It is quite safe. No camel will bite if it has a feedbag."

Haya notices how the Bedouin does not say "Your Royal Highness" when he speaks to her. He does not use her title like most people do, he says only her name. It is nice the way he says it, *Haya*, as if he were speaking to his own daughter, and it makes her feel at home, out here in the desert. And she is home. After all, she is a Bedouin too.

"Hello, Fluffy." Haya strokes the camel's soft caramel fur. How different the camel is to Bree, his face all velvet but lumpy-bumpy with stiff whiskery hair sprouting everywhere and those enormous brown eyes with long lashes, built to withstand the grit of a desert sandstorm.

"Haya!"

Haya raises her head at the sound of Ali's voice, but when she peers down the row of camels, she cannot see him anywhere.

"Ali?"

There is silence. No reply.

"Ali, where are you?"

Haya leaves Fluffy and Lulabelle and begins to walk along the camel row. Ali and his tricks! He must be hiding, nestled in beside one of the great beasts. She looks for him as she walks all the way down the row and back again, but there is no sign of her brother. Now she is becoming anxious.

"Ali?"

And then she hears a giggle. It sounds like it came from one of the camels.

Haya listens hard as she moves slowly from camel to camel. And then, when she is halfway along the row, she hears another giggle. The sound is muffled, but she can tell exactly where it is coming from.

Strapped to each saddle are two large bags made of brightly coloured canvas, each one big enough to hold all a Bedouin might need for months in the desert. If she looks closely, Haya can see that one of the bags is breathing in and out.

"Ali?" Haya gives the saddlebag a jab with her finger and the bag suddenly comes to life and begins to squirm. "Come out, I know you are in there."

Haya pokes the bag again and a mop of dark hair and two eyes pop up from the top of it.

"Let's play hide-and-seek," Ali says.

They spend the morning playing among the camels. Then, when they get thirsty, they go back into the tent for more tea and listen to the men telling their battle stories. The desert can be a dangerous place, full of bandits, and those daggers and the guns that the Desert Patrol carry are not just for show. Haya and Ali sit wide-eyed and listen to the tales until finally their father and Major Jafar both rise and signal to the men. It is time to go.

The camels' feedbags are gone and there are colourful bridles on their heads instead. One of the Bedouin is busy tightening Lulabelle's girth.

"She is ready for you, Haya," he says.

Haya steps up to the camel and the Bedouin takes his stick and taps the camel lightly behind the knee. "Cush, Lulabelle," he commands. "Cush."

Lulabelle brays her objection and refuses to drop, but the Bedouin is firm with her. "Cush!"

With a groan of resignation, Lulabelle drops to her knees and then lowers her hindquarters so that she is ready for Haya to climb aboard.

Haya has never ridden a camel before. The saddle is not like the ones that horses wear. It is made of hard wood with two very high pommels at the front and the back, and the seat is draped in a thick curly goat hide. When Haya is seated, she finds it surprisingly comfortable. She grabs the front pommel with one hand and the camel's rope with the other, and then the officer gives Lulabelle a tap on her flank and the camel rises. Haya gives a squeak of surprise as she suddenly finds herself up very high indeed, two metres above the sand.

"Use the rope or the stick to guide her. Tap her there on the flanks to make her go," Major Jafar says. And, with no more explanation, they are off, the King and Major Jafar leading the ride and Lulabelle falling to the rear of the camel train with Fluffy running loose at her heels as they set off across the desert.

The swaying motion of the camel feels like being on a boat cast adrift, rocking back and forth and side to side. It is so different to riding a horse; the camel's wide strides are so ponderous as they lumber across the sand. They make good progress though and soon they are deep into the desert, climbing up rocky pathways that the jeeps cannot travel.

Coming downhill, the desert beneath them stretches to the kingdom's border and the neighbouring dominion of Syria. Haya stares out across the parched, sun-bleached landscape and sees… nothing. Just sand and rocks and more desert, all the way to the horizon.

On the King's shoulder, the falcon too seems to be scanning the horizon – although this is impossible since the bird still wears his hood.

Suddenly there is a movement in a tussock ahead. The King sees it and signals for the party to halt. Alone, with Akhbar on his shoulder and Anber the saluki at his heels, he rides forward.

When the King halts his camel, the dog drops obediently to a crouch beside him. The hound is motionless; he waits patiently while the King lifts Akhbar to his fist and removes the falcon's hood so the bird can see.

Akhbar casts his eyes up at the blue sky, then scopes the desert terrain.

Whatever was moving out there before, Haya cannot see it. But the eyes of a girl are not those of a falcon. Akhbar has spied his prey: a desert hare, moving a hundred metres away.

Once, Haya had a conversation with her father about how much she disliked hunting. "It is cruel," she told him. "The poor hare gets killed."

"This is how the Bedouin, our ancestors, hunted for centuries," the King said. "It is not a sport for us, Haya, it is tradition, our way of life."

"But there are supermarkets now," Haya pointed out. "We could get a hare from there instead."

"And how did the hare in the supermarket get there?" her father asks.

The King holds Akhbar aloft and releases him. In two powerful beats of his great wings, the falcon lifts up and is gone. Haya shields her eyes and watches him soaring above the desert, his wings outstretched.

The falcon begins to circle, getting lower and lower. But he has lost sight of the hare. It has gone to ground and knows better than to move now. It will lie and wait.

The falcon cannot flush it out from his vantage point in the sky.

But the hare did not reckon on Anber.

The King whistles a command and the saluki, who has been resting patiently at the feet of his camel, springs forward, swift as a deer, running on velvet paws. It doesn't take him more than a few seconds to cover the ground to the tussock and once he catches the scent he hones in on the hare, chasing it out so that the prey is running in the open once more. Akhbar stoops and dives, his quarry in his sights.

Sensing the danger above, the hare springs forward, strong haunches powering it in rapid strides. Anber is giving chase, but the hare is even quicker. It darts ahead, always maddeningly out of reach of the saluki. The hare does not run in a straight line, but flits this way and that, hoping to confuse the hound so it can go to ground again.

If the saluki were hunting alone, then the hare's dramatic twists and turns would be enough to put him off the trail. But up above, Akhbar the falcon is following the hare too. Each time the hare changes direction, Akhbar swoops down directly above the prey, giving the dog a marker to follow.

The hare ducks and weaves, but it is beginning to flag.

It is accustomed to outrunning its foe with cleverness and very short bursts of speed. It should have been able to go to ground by now, but with the falcon circling above and the saluki below working in tandem, the hare is tiring fast.

Anber is gaining and as the hare tries to change course the hound puts on a burst of speed and outstrips his prey stride for stride. In a moment, the saluki is upon him. In a single swift move, he takes the hare in his mighty jaws and shakes it with an instinctive flick of his head, instantly snapping the neck.

With a shrill whistle, the King calls the hound back to him and Haya watches as the saluki drops the hare and obediently turns to go back to his master.

From the sky above, Akhbar plummets with his talons extended in front of him. Without touching the ground, the falcon swoops low enough to grasp the limp body of the hare in his claws. Then, with three massive beats of his powerful wings, he lifts up into the sky with the hare dangling beneath him.

The hare must weigh almost as much as Akhbar and he has to pound his wings to remain in the air. Anber races below him, but the falcon is swift. The hound has only just reached the King when there is a cry from

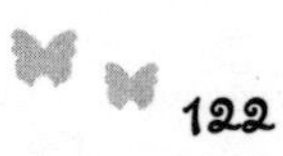

above as the falcon comes back down to earth, dropping the hare neatly at the feet of his master.

That night, back at the palace, Baba, Haya and Ali have wild hare stew for supper.

Chapter 9

Mrs Goddard and the Tanks

Santi has explained how the filly must be weaned and at eight months old he tells Haya it is time.

They do it first thing one morning. While Santi loads Latifah into the horse float, Haya does her best to distract Bree. It is all going smoothly until the float begins to leave the yard and Latifah cries out.

"It's OK, Bree, I am here, shhh." Haya tries to comfort her startled filly, but it is no good. Bree slams up against the stable door with her chest, trying to force her way free, desperate to be reunited with the grey mare. Her frantic whinnies fill the air as she cries out. Haya stands by helplessly, realising that nothing she can do will ease the pain.

When Santi returns to the yard, he finds Bree in a lather, her distraught cries still echoing round the yard and the young Princess slumped against the door of the loose box in a flood of tears.

"Dry your eyes, Titch," Santi tells her firmly. "You are in charge, remember? Sometimes we must do what is best for our horses, even though it hurts."

"It is too cruel," Haya says. "Look at her!"

"Her heartbreak will not last long," Santi reassures her. "Horses are luckier than us. They live in the now. They cannot cling to memories as we do."

Sure enough, two days later, Bree is quite content in her box on her own, and she is eating alfalfa and barley just like the grown-up polo mares.

Weaned off milk and on to hard feed, Bree grows quickly. Haya is growing too. At the stables she smiles and laughs with the grooms, singing songs as she helps them with the chores.

"What happened to our quiet girl?" Santi teases her. "Now we cannot get you to stop talking!"

*

On the first day when snow falls, Haya leads Bree out into the yard and watches to see what the filly will do. She remembers the way that Amina used to hate the feeling of the snowflakes on her face, how the mare would try and bury her head in Haya's coat to wipe them off. In contrast, Bree steps out eagerly, snorting and stamping at the snow flurries, as if she is trying to crush them beneath her hooves.

Haya takes her down to the polo training grounds to let her loose to stretch her legs. When she unclips the lead rope, Bree trots out into the middle of the field and then stops abruptly to give the snow a sniff, then digs a little hole with her front hoof before dropping to her knees to roll. Haya watches the filly grunting with delight as she merrily flings her legs in the air and rolls back and forth, relishing the feeling of the cold snow on her back. Although Bree may look like her mother, they are not the same horse at all.

Bree's coat has grown thick and shaggy like a teddy bear over the cold months, but as the snow melts, her fur begins to shed. And just like Amina, every time Haya grooms her, great clumps come out on the brushes to reveal a glossy bay summer coat underneath. Haya can see just how muscled and powerful her filly has become. Already at nearly two Bree is built like a showjumper, with well-rounded haunches and strong shoulders. Haya desperately wants to sit astride Bree, to ride with the wind in her hair, galloping across the desert sands.

"Bree is still not ready to break in," Santi tells her. "Why not ride one of the other horses?"

"I don't want to ride another horse, I want my horse."

"I understand, Titch," Santi nods. "But your filly must be given time to mature. It will be another year before you can break her in to the saddle. Use that time and become a rider. Then you will be ready for her."

"Who will I ride instead?" Haya asks.

Santi says, "We will put you on one of the Tanks."

The Tanks, two of them, live at the stables at Al Hummar. They are golden Palominos, sent to the King as a gift from America.

The Tanks came to Jordan by sea, many years ago, arriving at the port of Aqaba. When their ship dropped anchor, the horses had been standing in their crates on deck for so long they could barely move their legs and so Santi decided the best way to bring them ashore was to crane them over the railings and let them swim.

In the salt water, the horses' limbs loosened up and they snorted and churned their way through the waves. As they stepped out of the sea on to the pale sands, the grooms gathered round in amazement. They had never seen horses like these before. The Palominos were stocky and solid, with thick legs and barrel-bodies. Compared to the delicate, fine-boned Arabians of Al Hummar, they were enormous.

"These are not horses!" one of the grooms exclaimed. "They are tanks!" And so the nickname stuck.

The Tanks have a loose box each prepared for them at the polo stables. One Tank is for Haya and the other for Prince Hassan's daughter, Princess Badiya. It is decided that Ali can ride Dandy the Shetland and he is moved here too. Now the only thing missing is a teacher.

"Her name is Mrs Goddard," Prince Hassan tells the King. "She is an Englishwoman who has recently moved to Jordan with her husband. By all accounts she is an expert horsewoman and has volunteered her services."

The morning of their first riding lesson, Haya and Badiya and Ali all saddle up their horses with help from Prince Hassan's polo grooms.

The same age as Haya, Badiya is a delicate girl with wide eyes and thick jet-black hair to her waist. A beautiful and gracious child, she is every inch the Princess. As they stand and wait, Badiya makes pretty braids in her pony's mane and when she giggles Haya thinks how even Badiya's laugh is perfect, like the clear, crystal tinkle of a brook.

"Where is Mrs Goddard then?" Haya sighs. She is tired of waiting. She wants to ride.

"Why don't we get on?" she suggests to Badiya. "I'll leg you up if you like."

"OK," Badiya agrees.

Haya takes the Palomino's reins and puts them over the horse's neck. Then she grabs Badiya by the leg and flings her up into the saddle. Unfortunately she has grabbed the wrong leg and somehow Badiya ends up back to front, facing the tail.

"Climb back down!" Haya tells her.

"I can't!" Badiya squeaks.

"Jump down then!" Ali entreats.

This is the state that Mrs Goddard finds them in when she arrives. There is a lot of tutting and head-shaking as Mrs Goddard lifts Badiya back to earth. "Our first lesson today will be mounting the horse."

Despite the desert heat, Mrs Goddard is dressed in a tweed hacking jacket and banana yellow riding breeches that balloon over her thighs. She has a back like a ramrod and wears her coiffed hair like the Queen of England with a neat scarf tied under her chin. She wears a pair of spotless cream leather gloves and she carries a smart brown leather cane with a silver tip. The cane, Haya soon discovers, is an extension of Mrs Goddard's right hand – she uses it to gesticulate as she talks, thwacking it loudly against the side of her long leather boots.

"Riding," Mrs Goddard says as she marches up and down the yard in front of her young charges, "is a discipline that takes a lifetime to master."

"It feels like a lifetime already," Haya mutters under her breath to Badiya. Beside them, Ali stifles a giggle.

Haya cannot understand Mrs Goddard. She is supposed to be a riding instructor, but spends half an hour explaining the correct way to mount, before they are even allowed on to their ponies! Once they are actually onboard, things get even worse.

"Let us discuss the correct position in the saddle. There must be a straight line directly down through the shoulder, the hips and the ankle and another straight line from the elbow to the wrist and all the way to the bit on the bridle. Your reins are held between the ring finger and the little finger just so. Let me see your reins, Princess Haya. That's right."

"Mrs Goddard, when are we going to gallop?"

"Well, I can tell you it won't be today!"

"Mrs Goddard?"

"Yes, Princess Haya?"

"Can we ride like the Indians do in cowboy movies?"

"Cowboys and Indians?" Mrs Goddard is horrified. "Princess Haya, I am a certified British Horse Society instructor. This is not the Wild West!"

There are no more questions allowed during the lesson. The next hour is spent mounting and dismounting and checking their positions, and there is barely time to walk the ponies once round the arena before Mrs Goddard announces that is all for the day.

"I hope you appreciate this," Haya complains to Bree in her loose box once the instructor is gone. "I am doing this for you!"

She strokes the filly's muzzle. "I'm going to become a real rider, Bree," Haya whispers. "Then we will gallop across the desert together, you and me. And just let Mrs Goddard try to catch us!"

Haya's father has to go to London for a meeting and when he returns he brings presents for Haya, Ali and Badiya. The gifts are wrapped in paper from Harrods and when Haya unwraps hers she is delighted to own her first pair of proper jodhpurs. There is also a tweed hacking jacket and a velvet hard hat. Badiya is thrilled with her outfit and parades it in front of the mirror, but Haya just pulls on the jodhpurs and leaves the rest in the tissue paper.

"Do I have to wear these for lessons?" she asks her father. It is a bit much having a hacking jacket on in the hot sun and no one else in the yards wears a helmet.

"Mrs Goddard insists," the King says.

"Mrs Goddard is no fun. I shall be ninety years old by the time she lets me canter."

After her lessons with Mrs Goddard, Haya always lingers at the yards. She watches her uncle cantering his polo ponies in wide circles round the big arena at the bottom of the hill. Why can't she ride like that?

Most of the polo ponies in Prince Hassan's stables are mares, but there is one gelding. His name is Solomon and he is a deep, rich chestnut colour with a white blaze and two white socks. Solomon is quite tall for a polo pony, but he has deep brown eyes that are kind and gentle. He would be lovely to ride. One day, after the lesson with Mrs Goddard is over and the yards are quiet for once, Haya goes to the tack room and lifts down Solomon's bridle from its hook and heaves the saddle over her arm.

It is not easy for her to get the bridle on the big chestnut; she has to reach up very high to slip it over his ears. It is even harder to get the saddle on, but she manages somehow. She gets the girth good and tight round Solomon's belly and then leads him out into the yard and, using the box once more, she flings herself lightly into the saddle.

It is like being up a tall tower! Solomon is so much bigger than the Tanks and yet he's so skinny there is nothing to grasp between her legs. He has a long neck and it stretches in front of her like a giraffe.

"Good boy, Solly." Haya clucks the gelding on and he moves forward obediently. They walk down the rutted track that leads to the training field. Solomon has realised now that the lightweight on his back is not Prince Hassan, but he is a good-natured horse and he steps out willingly as Haya walks him back and forth across the sandy surface of the polo field.

"Good boy, Solomon, shall we try a trot?" Haya puts her legs on tight against Solomon's sides, as Mrs Goddard has taught her.

But Solomon is trained to break straight into a canter.

As the big chestnut surges forward, Haya gets the shock of her life. She is cantering! It feels so fast it is almost like they are flying across the field, and so smooth – not at all bouncy like a trot, but fluid, like riding a rocking horse. This is what she always dreamed it would be like, with the wind in her hair and a horse beneath her.

It is magical.

When Haya takes a pull on the reins, the enchantment comes abruptly to an end. Solomon gives a sudden pivot on his hindquarters. Haya lets out a shriek as she is flung forward on to his neck. She clings on for all she is worth, but it does no good and she is thrown out of the saddle. Solomon comes to a halt, but it is too late to save her. Haya slides in an undignified heap, landing on her bottom on the soft loam of the polo field.

She sits there panting with shock. She has never fallen off a horse before. The ground came up at her a lot faster than she expected! Once she gets her breath back though, she realises that falling isn't so bad. She isn't hurt at all. She gets up and dusts off her jodhpurs.

Solomon seems genuinely sorry that his overenthusiastic turn has thrown her off. He lowers his head to give her a sniff with nostrils open wide, as if to say, "Hey, what are you doing down there?"

"Good Solomon." Haya leads the big chestnut over to the railing, climbing up so that she can reach the stirrup with her foot and mount up again.

This time she doesn't pull at the reins with so much gusto. She turns Solomon gently, circling the field, getting a feel for the big horse's strides. Haya does not know it, but she rides exactly as Mrs Goddard would wish her to. She has perfect posture in the saddle, with her back straight, and her hands steady and poised in front of her.

She canters like this for almost an hour. When at last she rides Solomon back up the rutted track from the arena, she sees Prince Hassan looking down at her from the yards. She realises he has been standing there watching her the whole time.

As she rides Solomon back up the hill to join her uncle, Haya can feel her heart racing. Solomon is his favourite polo pony. She will be in big trouble for taking him.

"That was quite a fall you took," her uncle says. "Are you all right?"

"Yes, uncle."

"Are you sure?"

Haya nods.

"Good," Prince Hassan says. "You have only six more to go."

"Six more?" Haya asks.

"They say it takes seven falls before you can call yourself a rider," Hassan says. "I have fallen more than seven times myself, too many to count."

He smiles at Haya. "You had better ride Solomon

again tomorrow, eh?"

This is how Haya develops her skills, spending hours and hours cantering the big chestnut polo pony round and round the field. As the weeks go by, Hassan will occasionally come down to the fields and show her his polo tricks, how to use her reins to steer the horse by holding them against his neck, pushing him from side to side. Soon she can pull Solomon this way and that without ever losing a beat. She can canter like polo players do, rising up into the air on every second stride.

"No, no, no!" Mrs Goddard nearly has kittens when Haya tries the same thing in her riding lessons. "We are not in Argentina herding cattle like gauchos! I will not have you neck-reining your pony in my class. For heaven's sake, will you please sit down properly and stop using your stirrups to stand when you are cantering! This is not a polo chukka!"

Mrs Goddard might lose her temper, but she cannot deny that Haya is her star pupil. With each day, her balance and skill are growing. By the time winter has been and gone and the spring is in bloom she is able to ride Solomon at a gallop bareback and coax the horse into twists and turns on the polo field, barely touching the reins. Solomon is too tall for her to practise vaulting tricks so when she wants to play cowboys and Indians and leap onboard at a gallop she rides the Tank.

She is learning to jump too – Mrs Goddard makes her stick to trotting poles and cavaletti in her lessons, but when her instructor's back is turned, she jumps everything and anything in her path. Old forty-four-gallon drums, sacks of barley and packing crates all become show jumps to ride the Tank over. Haya imagines that she is showjumping at the Horse of the Year Show with the roar of the crowd in her ears just like she has seen on the TV.

She rides other horses in the stables too, and is learning how to be sensitive as a rider and accommodate their quirks. Santi tells her it is good training to ride as many horses as possible to develop your instinct and feel. Haya knows this is important because the horse that she plans to ride is not Solomon or the Tank. Her heart remains set on the pretty bay filly with one white sock and a white star on her forehead, who whinnies when Haya comes to visit her loose box each morning.

Bree is well past three years old now and she has yet to feel the weight of a rider on her back. She has never had a bit between her teeth or felt the girth tighten round her as the saddle is strapped on.

All that is about to change. It is time to break her in.

Chapter 10

The Dumb Waiter

"Princess Haya, would you please pass me the oyster fork?"

Haya sighs and looks down at the table. Laid out in front of her is the Royal Jordanian dinner service, each plate adorned with the crest and initials of the King, and beside it a long row of exquisite silver cutlery. It is just like a state dinner – except there is no food being served, and there are no guests in the room, just Haya and Frances.

The Princess looks at the six forks in front of her. She takes a guess and picks up the skinniest one with two pointy prongs.

"That is a snail fork," Frances says with an air of

despair. "The oyster fork is to the left of it. It has the three tines, do you see? The wide one at the side severs the oyster from its shell and then you use the slender tines to spear the oyster and carry it to your mouth…"

"But I don't like oysters," Haya says.

"That," Frances replies, "is not the point. What if you are invited to a state dinner where oysters are served and you do not know which fork to use?"

"It won't matter because I won't be eating them." Haya feels as if Frances is missing the point here.

"You mother Queen Alia had the most noble manners." Frances busies herself rearranging the cutlery. "But then I suppose some apples do not fall so close to the tree."

Frances smooths down the tablecloth primly and then clasps both hands together and looks up gravely at the young Princess. "Now tell me. Which piece of cutlery would one use for eating strawberries?"

There was a time at Al Nadwa palace when Haya could practise her cartwheels up and down the corridors and get muddy running around on the lawn playing football with Ali and no one said anything about having to be proper and ladylike. But now she is ten she is being given cutlery classes.

"It's ridiculous," Haya grumbles to Ali as she rifles through the cutlery drawers in the royal kitchen. "Frances acts as if the kingdom will rise and fall on my ability to recognise forks!" She grasps two spoons and passes one to Ali and then opens the freezer and scans the shelves. Finally she sees the tub of strawberry ice cream. Ismail must have shoved it to the back of the shelf to hide it from her. She takes the tub and digs out two big servings of it, one for her and one for Ali. Then she gets out the chocolate sprinkles.

"I've tried to explain." Haya is shaking the sprinkles a little too vigorously and they fly all over the bench. Ali reaches out to grasp his bowl of ice cream, but Haya is not finished yet. "I told her that Bree is ready to be broken in now. She needs me. I should be at the stables – not stuck here!"

Haya absent-mindedly passes Ali his bowl. "Well, I don't care what Frances says. I am going to be a champion showjumper and I will live with my horses and I won't have a governess and no one will tell me what to do!"

Ali takes his bowl of ice cream and climbs up next to Haya on the kitchen bench. "I'm going to be a footballer," he tells her. "And a soldier."

"You might end up being a King," Haya points out.

"Like Baba."

"Nah," Ali says, swinging his legs over the edge of the bench. "Abdullah will be King."

Haya and Ali have a much older brother from the King's previous marriage.

"What about you?" Ali counters. "You might be a Queen."

Like Mama.

Haya knows that is what her brother was about to say, but he doesn't because talking about Mama always ends up with one of them getting upset.

"Uh-uh. I won't be a Queen," Haya says, "because I am never getting married. I am going to live with my horses instead." She puts on a posh voice as she mocks Frances: "*A Queen has noble manners. A Queen knows which one the oyster fork is.*"

They are on to their second bowl of ice cream when Zuhair, the head of the Royal Household, finds them in the kitchen.

"Frances is looking for you," he tells Haya. "Your violin tutor has been waiting for nearly half an hour."

Haya doesn't feel like playing her violin. "Can't we stay here?" she pleads with Zuhair. The kitchen is her favourite place to hide when Frances is on the warpath.

Frances may have her allies in the palace, but the kitchen staff and the waiters are like family to Haya and Ali. Zuhair, too, is always on their side. But today he shakes his head.

"You had better do as she says. The cooks won't want you underfoot when they are working."

There is a royal banquet on tonight and very soon Ismail and his team will be in to begin preparations for the meal. Ismail gets very grumpy when there are guests coming, and Haya decides she is better off facing Frances and the violin teacher.

Haya also has a tutor for singing and ballet, and a teacher who comes three times a week to improve her Arabic. Frances is in charge of the rest of her lessons. She teaches her maths and geography and English. When Haya's father was a boy, he went to boarding school in England. Frances says that in England you receive the finest education and one day Haya and Ali shall go too. As much as Haya cannot stand Frances, she thinks being sent to boarding school, away from Baba and Ali, would be much worse.

That evening Haya and Ali sit upstairs on the landing outside her room and watch the guests arriving in the entrance hall. The men are all dressed in dinner suits and

some of them wear military sashes.

Haya and Ali are eating in their rooms tonight and the meals are sent up to them in the dumb waiter, which is a very tiny elevator for food that travels up and down from the kitchen to the landing outside Haya's bedroom.

Haya loves to use the dumb waiter. She likes to put the tray inside and press the button to send it back to the kitchen once she has eaten. It is like a magic trick the way the tray goes into the box and then, *abracadabra*, Haya opens the roller door a few moments later and the dirty plates have disappeared.

For dinner the kitchen sends up plates of delicious hummus and tabbouleh salads with pitta bread for Haya and Ali. After they have eaten, they put the trays in the dumb waiter and send the plates back down. They play paper-scissors-rock to see who is going to press the button and Haya wins. Ali is annoyed because it was really his turn, and when the dumb waiter returns empty, he has an idea. He races into Haya's bedroom and retrieves Doll.

"We can put Doll in the dumb waiter," he says. "We can send her down to the kitchen and then get her back again."

Haya is not certain that she wants to put her old favourite dolly in the dumb waiter. She has a better idea.

"You get in," she says to Ali. "I will push the button and send you down to the kitchen."

"Me?" Ali squeaks.

"It can be our secret elevator," Haya tells him. "We can go down to the kitchen any time we want and get ice cream and no one can stop us!"

Ali is keen, but when Haya slides the roller door open, he hesitates.

"Come on! Get in!" Haya tells him. Her eyes are shining with excitement.

It is a small space, but he will fit if he curls up. "I don't want to do it," Ali says.

"Ali," Haya says. "You remember that time you asked me to help you to steal Baba's car so you could enter the driving rally?"

Ali nods.

"And I did it, didn't I?"

"Yeah," Ali looks uncertain, "but you crashed it into a wall…"

"But it worked out OK in the end," Haya insists. "Honestly, you'll be fine. You can't crash in a dumb waiter."

Ali is still grumbling as he squeezes inside and tucks up into a ball so that Haya can close the door.

"I'm going to press the button," Haya tells him. "When you get to the other end, knock on the roof of the box and I will hear you. I'll press it again and bring you back up."

"Should I open the door at the other end?" Ali asks.

"No," Haya tells him. "The kitchen will be too busy. We don't want Ismail to see you. Just knock on the roof and I will bring you straight back up again, OK?"

"OK," Ali agrees. He takes a deep breath as if he is about to be submerged underwater and Haya slides the roller door shut and presses the button. With a creak and a groan, the dumb waiter begins to move. Haya has never noticed quite how slow and noisy the thing is, but now that Ali is inside and she is waiting for it to reach the bottom it seems to be taking forever!

Downstairs at the dinner the guests have been served and Haya can hear their voices and the chink of knives and forks against the plates. She sticks her head back into the shaft. What is taking so long? Then she hears a heavy *thunk*. She peers into the darkness.

Bang, bang! It is Ali knocking on the box.

Haya slides the roller door shut and presses the button. The dumb waiter creaks into gear once more. It begins to move, slower than before, the pulley ropes groaning and whining. And then, with a shudder, the dumb waiter stops. This is not good. Haya presses the button again. Her fingers stab it a third time, then a fourth, but nothing happens.

Haya slides the roller door open and looks down the shaft. The pulleys should be grinding and turning, lifting the box back up to her, but they aren't moving.

"Ali?" she shouts down the shaft.

Inside the box, Ali has begun to panic. "Haya! Stop being silly! Make it come up! Haya!"

"Ali!" She calls back down the shaft to him. "Wait! It's stuck! I am going to get you out! Just stay there!"

She realises as she races down the stairs that her last words were pointless. Where else can Ali go? He is trapped inside the dumb waiter, wedged in the narrow shaft between the floors of the house.

Haya feels her heart pounding. The pulley ropes did not look very sturdy. What if they break? She has to find Zuhair.

Haya is almost at the kitchen when she hears the ominous clack of sensible heels behind her in the corridor. "Your Royal Highness?"

Oh no! Frances.

"Where are you going? You know you are not allowed

in the kitchen when there is a dinner party under way."

The lump in Haya's throat is now threatening to choke her. "I, ummm, I left Doll in the kitchen," she says. "I need to get her."

It is not the best excuse in the world, but luckily Frances accepts it.

"Very well, but stay out of the way," she says. "Get your doll and go straight back upstairs to bed."

"Yes, Frances!" Haya is already off and running for the kitchen. Ali has been in the dumb waiter for at least two minutes and he is probably starting to wonder if Haya has forgotten about him!

In the kitchen, the clattering pots and pans are so noisy it is no wonder the chefs haven't heard the knocking and cries of the nine-year-old boy stuck in the dumb waiter. But when Haya bursts in through the doors, Zuhair knows immediately that something is very wrong.

"It's Ali," Haya says, pushing up the roller door and sticking her head into the shaft. "He's stuck in there."

Zuhair looks at her wide-eyed in disbelief. "Prince Ali is inside the dumb waiter?"

"Yes!" Haya says.

"How did he get in there?" Zuhair asks.

"I put him in there!" Haya says with exasperation. "Only he was too heavy and it got stuck on the way back up."

The whole kitchen has stopped work. The pots and the pans are silent as the kitchen staff realise what is happening. The Prince of Jordan is stuck in a tiny wooden box dangling precariously by a rope and pulley.

Zuhair puts his head in the shaft and looks up. He can see the dumb waiter, stuck about halfway up. He tries pressing the button on the wall in the kitchen. Nothing happens.

One of the kitchen porters stands by nervously. "Mr Zuhair," he says. "Do you want me to fetch the King?"

"No!" Haya says. "Please! Don't tell my father." She looks up at Zuhair. "Help me to get him out!"

Zuhair takes a deep breath. Then he turns back to his staff. "You – go upstairs now!" he commands. "And you, go with him! See if you can work the pulleys by hand and lower the box back down. Be very careful!"

Haya suddenly looks worried. "Do you think Ali has enough air? Can he breathe?"

Her question is answered by vigorous thumping from inside the dumb waiter. "Let me out!" Ali shouts. "Haya! What's going on?"

"Ali!" Haya calls back up the shaft to him. "It's OK. Zuhair is fixing it. We're going to get you out."

Zuhair sticks his head up the shaft. "Stay very still, Ali!" he calls out. "We are trying to lower you down."

It seems to take forever for the porters to reach the top floor, and then ages for them to get the pulley moving, but eventually they manage to make the gears turn manually and the dumb waiter lowers slowly back down the shaft.

"Wait!" Zuhair cautions Ali as the dumb waiter comes to rest. But, as soon as the gap is wide enough, Ali squirms through it and Zuhair grabs him tight in his arms and pulls him to safety.

Then Zuhair rounds on Haya. "That," he tells her, "was a very foolish mistake."

"It was a test run," Haya says. "I was here to get help if anything went wrong."

Ali grins. "That was fun. Can we try it again?"

Before Zuhair can answer, the kitchen door swings open. It is Frances.

"What is going on in here?"

Haya's heart is racing. The kitchen staff do not say a word. Neither does Zuhair. He gives Haya a faint smile and she knows by the look in his eyes that he will keep this secret between them.

"Well?" Frances says, addressing them with an imperious tone. "Doesn't anyone have anything to say?"

The room is silent. And then, from the floor above them, a voice echoes down through the chamber of the dumb waiter. "Mr Zuhair! Did you get Prince Ali out yet?" There is a pause and then it gets worse as the porter's voice echoes again. "You better hurry up, Mr Zuhair! Frances is on her way to the kitchen…"

His voice is cut off mid-stream as Frances walks briskly across the room and slams down the door of the dumb waiter. Her face is full of fury as she turns on Haya and Ali.

Chapter 11

Taming the Wind

Haya climbs up on to the windowsill and dangles her legs over the edge. Her bedroom is on the second floor and it is a long way to the ground.

"Haya," Ali says anxiously. "Maybe we shouldn't do this."

"If you don't want to come, then stay home," Haya says. "I can go on my own." She shimmies out further on to the ledge and turns round so that she is facing the bedroom. Then, before Ali can say anything more, she drops from the windowsill and disappears into thin air.

"Haya!"

There is a fire escape about a metre below the sill and Haya lands on this and crouches low just out of his view.

When Ali sticks his head out of the window looking for her, Haya is there smiling up at him.

"Gotcha," she grins.

"Not funny," Ali insists.

"Come on, Ali!" Haya taunts him. "You're not scared, are you?"

"No," Ali says indignantly. "But we're already grounded for a month. If Frances catches us again..."

"She won't," Haya says emphatically. "Ali, I can't just leave Bree at the stables alone."

The filly is supposed to be broken in this week. Haya has promised that she'll behave and work hard at her lessons and never, ever leave the house, except to go to the stables and see her horse. But Frances knows that the best way to punish Haya is to keep her away from Bree, and has refused to let her see the filly.

"I'm sure Señor Lopez will have his grooms take care of the pony while you are grounded. There's no need for you to go anywhere near the stables."

The fire escape is like a jungle gym. The last rung is two metres off the ground and Haya hangs by her arms and then drops. Ali follows, landing on his feet like a cat, and together they walk to the gates of Al Nadwa.

The guards at the gate are surprised to see the

King's son and daughter walking alone without their bodyguards. Haya gives them a confident wave.

"Excuse me, Your Royal Highness?" It is one of the guards. "Where is your security detail?"

"It's OK," Haya smiles brightly. "We are only going to the stables."

She takes a few more steps and then the guard strides briskly after her. "Wait!" Haya stops and turns back to him. "I am not supposed to let you pass without a guard to accompany you."

Haya knew this was coming. "Please," she begs him. "I need to go and see my horse. Frances won't let me."

The guard looks worried. "Wait a moment."

He walks back to his post and speaks with the second guard and then he returns once more to Haya's side.

"Your Royal Highness," he says, "I have served your father for many years. Your mother, Queen Alia, was very good to me. Once, when my wife was ill and in great pain, it was the Queen who came to our house and nursed her and took her to hospital…" The guard looks misty-eyed, lost in the memory. Then he pulls himself together. "If your mother were here, she would not allow you and Prince Ali to travel the road to the stables alone…"

Haya is crestfallen until the guard adds, "But perhaps I could accompany you to the stable gates to make certain you arrive safely?"

*

Heat waves shimmer on the road and Haya and Ali are thirsty by the time they reach the stables. Haya goes into the tack room and gets them both a can of fizzy drink out of the fridge and they go to Bree's loose box.

"Bree? Bint Al-Reeh!" Haya calls.

At the sound of Haya's voice, Bree thrusts her head over the loose-box door and whinnies madly to her.

"Hey, girl." Haya strokes the filly as she unbolts the door and manoeuvres into the stall beside her. She slips on Bree's halter and begins to undo the straps on her stable rug.

Ali hangs off the stable door and watches as Haya moves expertly, always talking to her filly, her movements spare and unhurried. Haya keeps her body close to the filly as she leads her out into the yard. Bree is all keyed up and full of energy; she high-steps beside Haya, her breath coming in short, vibrating snorts, her eyes wide.

"It's OK, Bree, I'm here…"

The polo mares stick their heads out over the doors to see what all the fuss is about. Their attentions only make

Bree even more excited and she begins to dance. Haya keeps a firm hand on Bree's lead rein, using her voice to calm her.

"She looks scary," Ali says. He is at least three metres away and reluctant to come closer as Bree frets and stamps.

"She's just a little fresh," Haya says, undaunted. "Come on."

They walk down the track to the polo field, the filly springing off the ground as if there were hot coals beneath her hooves, tail high and neck arched. Haya walks Bree out on to the soft loam of the field and brings her to a halt near the wooden bench seats.

"What are you going to do?" Ali asks.

The truth is Haya has no idea how to break in a horse. She was supposed to take Bree to Al Hummar where there is a round pen and Santi and his grooms would be there to help her. But Frances ruined that plan. So now Haya is all on her own, trying to break in her filly on the wide-open polo field.

"I'm going to ride her," Haya says. She feels the hairs rise on the back of her neck. "Here, come and hold her steady for me."

Ali takes the lead rope with both hands and hangs on to Bree as if he were anchoring a ship while Haya climbs on to the bench seats.

Steadying herself, Haya prepares to jump. She feels like there should be something – a speech or at least a drum roll to signify the momentous nature of this occasion. *She is going to ride Bree.* Her horse whom she raised from a three-day-old foal. They are about to become united, two spirits joined as one at last.

Haya takes a deep breath and in one swift, catlike leap she throws herself on to Bree's back. Beneath her, the filly feels the sudden weight, a strange sensation she has never experienced before, and her muscles tense.

"It's me, Bree," Haya reassures her with her voice. "It's OK..." And then Bree starts to buck.

The filly bucks hard and fast, springing up on all four legs at once, doubling over beneath Haya, her feet pronging off the ground. Bree twists in midair as she goes up again and Haya loses her balance and begins to slip. It is the third buck that gets her. Haya is flung up and catapults through the air, then she hits the ground with such force that the wind is knocked clean out of her. She has never been winded before and it is the most horrible feeling. Shuddering and choking, she struggles to get the air back into her lungs, kneeling on all fours and gasping like a fish out of water. Ali runs to her side and asks if she is OK, but she can't speak. The shock makes her begin to cry and now her sobs are choking her as she tries to breathe.

"Haya?" Ali is wide-eyed. "Are you all right? Haya?"

Haya brushes the sand off her jodhpurs. Why won't her hands stop shaking? None of this is how it was supposed to be…

"She threw you really hard like a bucking bronco," Ali says.

Haya brushes away her tears. Hateful, childish tears! She is supposed to be a rider and here she is on the ground crying like a little kid.

"I'm OK," she tells Ali. Even though she is upset and shaken, Haya knows what she must do. She has to get back on the horse.

"Haya…"

Exasperated, Haya turns to her brother. "What is it?"

Ali points up the hill at the men who are walking swiftly down from the polo stables towards them. There are six security guards, including the guard that she spoke to at the gate who walked with them. The guards are striding towards them with a sense of purpose and at the centre of the group, looking very serious, is her father, the King.

"Baba is here," Ali says.

In the car on the short journey back to Al Nadwa, her father, surprisingly, is not angry.

"No," he tells Haya, "I am disappointed."

Disappointed. The word cuts Haya like a knife.

"You left the house without a bodyguard, and without telling anyone," the King continues, "got on an unbroken horse by yourself—"

"But I wasn't by myself," Haya says. "Ali was with me. And this is Frances's fault! She wouldn't let me see Bree…"

"Haya," her father says. "Do you know why you got in trouble when you put your brother in the dumb waiter?"

"Because I got caught," Haya says.

The King shakes his head. "Because what you did was dangerous. Ali could have been injured. And today, when you climbed out of the fire escape and left the house without your bodyguard, you put yourself in danger."

"I'm sick of having guards following me around all the time. I can look after myself," Haya asserts.

"Haya, it is in your nature to be bold. It's an admirable quality. But please do not be naïve. You are the daughter of a King and a member of the Royal Hashemite clan of Jordan. When you disobey the rules and sneak out of the house alone, then you risk your life and your brother's too. What would I do if you were kidnapped or worse?"

The King takes his daughter's hand. "You and Ali are the precious gifts that your mother left behind. I will do whatever I must to keep you safe. Do you understand?"

The mention of Mama makes Haya's eyes prick with tears. She never meant to upset her father, not like this.

"Yes, Baba," Haya says, feeling the weight of his words. And then she adds, "Please don't let the guard at the gate get into trouble because of this. It was my fault. I made him let us past."

There is silence in the car, then the King sighs. "No one is in trouble. And I think it is best if I get Santi to move the filly back to Al Hummar. From what I saw of your antics today, I would prefer it if he were there to help you from now on. You are supposed to be breaking a horse, not your neck."

Haya's heart skips. "I can go there? To Al Hummar? I can break her?"

"If you try to go out again without a bodyguard, then you will be grounded for two months," the King says, "but yes, I am allowing you to go to the stables to break in the filly."

*

When Haya arrives at Al Hummar the following day, Santi is waiting for her with his music blaring from the record player and the smell of cardamom coffee filling his office.

"Your father tells me that you tried to ride her by yourself?" Santi says.

"She bucked me off," Haya tells him. "I thought she would let me ride her, but she was totally wild and acted like she didn't even know me."

Santi considers this. "Titch," he says, "come and stand behind me."

Haya is puzzled, but she does as he asks.

"You see the chair there next to you?" Santi says. "Get up on it."

Haya clambers up on the chair. "Now," Santi says, leaning over in front of her, "leap on to my back."

Santi has gone mad! But Haya does as he says. She jumps off the chair on to his back so that now he is piggybacking her.

"Now," Santi says, "imagine I am Bree. I cannot see you. I do not know that it is you, Haya, on my back. For all I know, you are a mountain lion who has pounced, for this is exactly how a big cat might attack. So I am thinking that any moment now you are about to unleash

your claws and tear me apart. How can I possibly get rid of you?"

Haya suddenly feels very foolish. "You can buck me off," she says.

Santi stands up straight and Haya slides down off his back. "Do not be discouraged, Titch," he says. "The filly loves you very much, but love will not stop her from giving in to instinct. When you jumped on her back on the polo field, you took her by surprise. She did the only thing she could do to protect herself."

Haya thinks about Bree, the way the filly was still trembling with fear after she had thrown her to the ground. "It was my fault," she says. "I scared her."

"Never mind," Santi says firmly. "That is the past and now we start again."

He smiles at Haya. "First she learns to take the bit in her mouth, then she feels the girth round her belly and saddle on her back. And then, finally, the rider."

"How long will it take?" Haya asks.

"Patience is what you need for breaking in horses, Titch," Santi says. "It will take as long as it takes."

*

In the yards at Al Hummar, the head groom Yusef waves to her. "Princess Haya, you are back!" he grins. "You have come to help me clean out the loose boxes maybe?"

"Not today, Yusef," Haya smiles.

Santi has put Bree back in her old loose box to the left-hand side of the first courtyard. When Haya arrives at her stall, there is already a groom in there with the filly, mucking out the damp straw into a wheelbarrow. He is not much older than she is, with a lean build, black hair and grey eyes. At the sight of Haya looking over the stable door, his grey eyes go wide, like a hare that has just spied a falcon.

"Hello, I'm Haya."

The boy looks shocked. He makes a clumsy attempt at a bow. "I know, Your Royal Highness."

"Has Bree settled in OK?"

"Bree?" The boy looks terrified.

"That's my nickname for her," Haya says, looking at the bay filly standing at the back of the loose box.

"Oh, yes, Bint Al-Reeh is very settled, Your Royal Highness."

"And how long have you been here for?" Haya asks the boy.

"One month," he says. "I mean, one month – Your Royal Highness."

"How old are you?"

"Fourteen, Your Royal Highness."

"And what is your name?"

"Zayn, Your Royal Highness."

"Zayn, you don't have to say Your Royal Highness in every sentence when you speak to me, you know."

"Yes, Your Royal Highness. I mean, no, Your Royal Highness. I mean – yes!" Zayn is so flustered he looks overwhelmed with relief when Santi comes to take Bree to the round pen.

"The new groom is strange," Haya tells Santi once they are alone with Bree. "I don't think he likes me."

"Zayn?" Santi smiles. "He is daunted by you."

"Why?"

"Because he has never met the daughter of a King before."

*

Haya is expecting Santi to enter the round pen with her, but instead, he leans on the railings giving instructions while Haya handles Bree on her own.

Today she is teaching Bree to wear a bridle. The filly is accustomed to a halter, but the bridle is new. As Haya slips the reins over Bree's head and then lifts the bridle headpiece up to the filly's muzzle, Bree pulls her head away.

"It's OK," Santi says. "Try holding one arm round her muzzle as you lift the bridle up."

Bree keeps her head still as Haya works her fingers to ease open the corners of Bree's mouth. After a couple of attempts, she manages to open the filly's jaw enough to slip the bit in. Haya does up the straps while Bree champs and frets at the new sensation of the metal bit.

"That is quite normal, a good response," Santi reassures Haya.

After a few minutes, Haya takes the bridle off and then tries putting it on again. This time the filly does not make a fuss about accepting the bit. "That is very good," Santi says. "Take it off again and she can go back to the loose box – that is all for today."

Haya is surprised. They have been in the round pen for less than half an hour. "We break in a horse without a battle," Santi says. "Quiet and slow. Put her back in the box and give her some feed – let her know that she has been a good horse."

The next day at the round pen they put on the bridle again. Bree still champs at the metal, but she is quite relaxed so Santi says she is ready for the saddle blanket. "Remember that anything on their back is a lion," Santi reminds her. "Show her she is safe. Rub her down with

the saddle blanket to show it will not hurt her."

At first, Bree tenses her muscles, but Haya stays calm, stroking her shoulders and neck with the cloth, persisting until the mare settles. Very soon Bree does not even flinch when Haya vigorously flicks the blanket over her hindquarters.

"Very good." Santi leans over the railing of the round pen watching them. "Make a fuss of her and take her back to the stables."

*

The next day the routine is the same once more and Haya thinks that Santi will call it quits when Bree walks calmly with the saddle blanket on her back, but instead, he says, "I think she is ready for the saddle."

The saddle is an English one, very old and made of hard brown leather. It is quite heavy and Haya struggles to lift it on to Bree's back. When she feels the weight on top of her, Bree collapses forward, as if she is about to drop to her knees, with a queer look on her face, giving throaty snorts. Haya keeps a hand on the filly's neck and keeps talking to her the whole time, reassuring her. Then, carefully, she reaches under Bree's belly and grasps the girth – slowly, gently – and raises it and does up the straps.

"Take the girth up another hole. Make it tight enough so that it won't slip," Santi advises. "OK, now knot the reins on her neck and let her go."

Bree lunges forward in a rush, thinking she can get away from the saddle by outrunning it. When the saddle stays firm on her back, Bree shakes her head and gives a half-hearted buck, attempting to dislodge the strange beast. But when that doesn't work, she simply accepts the saddle and begins to trot round the pen. "See how she tests the boundaries and then quickly she understands?" Santi says to Haya. "She is smart, even for an Arabian."

"Shall we take her back and untack her?" Haya asks.

"No." Santi shakes his head. "Today I think you should ride her. Look how calm she is. She is ready to be ridden."

The other grooms have gathered to watch Santi and Haya. Along with Yusef there is Radi, the slightly-built groom, and Attah, a Bedouin with bandy legs from spending all his life in the saddle. They lean against the fence with the new groom Zayn.

Haya should feel nervous with all these eyes on her. But the strange thing is, once she steps out into the round pen, the world slips away. It is just her and her horse. Bree walks up to Haya and thrusts her nose into the girl's chest as if to say, "Thank goodness you're here! There's this thing stuck on my back..."

Haya whispers private words to Bree as she moves all around her, stroking her coat, letting the filly feel her touch. Then she reaches her arms across the saddle and bounces up off her feet, resting a little of her weight on Bree's back. She stays up there for a moment, then drops lightly back to the ground. Bree seems quite happy so Haya tries again, only this time she lies right across the saddle and keeps her weight there. Her body is draped across the saddle, as if she were a sack of grain slung on to the back of a mule.

Bree turns her head round to sniff at Haya as if to say, "Hello! What are you doing there?" Her eyes are inquisitive and her lips take a friendly nibble at Haya's long dark hair. Haya smiles and runs her hand over the filly's shoulders.

"I think I could try sitting up on her now," Haya says. "Should I do it?"

"You know her best," Santi says. "Trust your instincts."

If she tries to sit up too soon, Bree will panic and buck like she did on the polo field. Haya will end up on the floor of the round pen and all her hard work of the past weeks will be undone.

"What do you think, Bree?" she whispers. "Are you ready?"

Haya braces her forearms, grasping the front and back of the saddle in each hand before smoothly kicking up her right leg and swinging it neatly across Bree's rump. And there she is, sitting up in the saddle, astride her horse again.

And this time everything is different. Haya sits up tall on Bree's back and she feels the very last thing that a rider on an unbroken horse should. She feels safe. Bree sniffs Haya's foot in the stirrup as if to say, "Now what are you doing sitting up there?"

Haya strokes her neck. "I'm not going to hurt you," she reassures the filly. "We're just going for a little ride. A few steps, Bree, that's all."

The filly walks stiffly at first, as if she is holding her breath, but in just one lap of the round pen, it is as if she barely notices she has a rider on her back. When Haya puts her legs ever so lightly against Bree's sides, the filly reacts on cue, moving forward at a trot, her head held erect with ears pricked forward, her thick black tail raised high so that it streams out behind her. Haya rises easily in time with the filly's rhythm, and then, when Bree is ready, with her heart pounding, Haya sits deep in the saddle and clucks with her tongue. Then Bree canters.

Bree's canter is delicate and light as air. Haya closes her eyes, feeling the strides come like waves beneath her.

To break a horse in is something many riders dream of their whole lives. At just eleven years old Haya has done it all on her own. She is the first, the only person, ever to ride this filly. She has tamed the wind.

*

"Baba!" Haya runs through the doors of Al Nadwa, her face flushed with excitement. She cannot wait to tell her father about it.

As she runs through the corridors beneath the portraits of the Kings, her heart is soaring and she breaks into a grin when she catches sight of Ali running towards her.

"Ali! I did it! I rode her. Where is Baba?"

"Baba is in the Blue Room," Ali says.

Then Haya registers the look on Ali's face. "What is it? Is something wrong?"

"I heard Baba talking to Frances."

"What about? Ali? Tell me!"

"They are sending you away!" Ali's voice is trembling. His face is streaked with tears.

"Haya, you are going to boarding school."

CHAPTER 12

A Strange Land

"This is all because I stuck Ali in the dumb waiter?" Haya fights to hold back the tears.

"Of course not, Haya," her father says.

"Then it's because Frances told you how I tried to slide down the banisters?" Haya sniffs. "I was totally safe. I wore my riding helmet."

"Actually," her father says, "I didn't know about that particular incident."

He takes Haya in his arms. "You haven't done anything wrong. We've talked about this, and the time is here now. You are eleven years old, and your future lies ahead of you. It is my responsibility to prepare you for it as best I can and the best schooling I can give you is in England."

This is the tradition. Her Baba went to Harrow and Sandhurst and Mama went to school in London. Now it is Haya's turn to be educated abroad.

"Please, Baba," Haya begs. "I'll do everything Frances says – I'll study hard and do all my homework. I want to stay here with you and Ali."

"I want you to stay with me too," the King says. "But I cannot keep you here. I must do what is right. Frances says that you are doing well in your studies, but you need specialist teachers in science and mathematics and languages. You passed your eleven-plus with excellent marks. You should be very proud of being accepted. Badminton is a very good school."

"What about Bree?" Haya sniffles.

"They have an excellent equestrian department at Badminton."

Haya perks up. "So I could take her with me?"

"No," the King says. "But there will be other horses that you can ride."

"I don't want another horse," Haya says. "I don't want to go."

*

Boarding school begins in September, which means Haya has three months left at Al Nadwa. She clings on to the days, trying to keep them alight like candles, to make them burn forever, but time keeps moving and she cannot stop it. So she spends every possible moment that she can with Bree. As soon as Frances releases her from her lessons, she goes straight to the stables.

Most days when she arrives, Zayn is there in Bree's loose box. She has told him loads of times that she can do it herself, but he always mucks out for her before she comes. He grooms Bree too, and the filly's fine bay coat has a sheen that Haya has never seen before.

"How do you get her so glossy?" she asks. And Zayn shyly shows her the wisp he has made out of hay. "You use it like this," he says, massaging the filly in vigorous circles.

"Who taught you how to make hay wisps?"

"My father, Your Royal Highness. He taught me everything about horses. He told me once that all Circassians can ride from the day we are born. We are natural horsemen."

"Does your father have many horses?"

"My father died when I was seven years old," Zayn says and his voice weakens and becomes so quiet that Haya can hardly hear him. "He was killed in Black September."

Haya feels his grief connect with her like a sharp pain in her belly. "I am so sorry," she says. "You must miss him so much."

Zayn takes a deep breath and when he speaks again his voice is strong once more. "My mother says that my father would be very proud that I work in the King's stables. I live with her and my two sisters and the money from my wages keeps all of us."

He digs about in the back pocket of his trousers and produces a worn leather wallet. He opens it to show Haya the photo inside.

"That is my mother there and those are my sisters," Zayn says. "They're both at school now. They were only babies when my father died…"

Haya looks at the photograph. "Your mother is very beautiful," she tells Zayn and without thinking she begins to speak of her own mother too. "There are lots of photographs of my mother in the palace. Baba tells me stories about her. I think about her all the time, but... I cannot really remember her, not properly."

It is the first time that Haya has admitted this to herself, let alone out loud, and somehow it feels like a tiny bit of pressure has lifted.

"I remember my father," Zayn says. "I don't know if

that's better or worse."

He looks at Haya, and his grey eyes are filled with the sadness of loss. "I didn't think you'd be like this," he says.

"Like what?"

"Like a… real person."

Haya raises her hand and strokes Bree's muzzle. "That is why I love it so much here. The horses do not care that I am a Princess. And Santi and Yusef, they pass me a broom and ask me to clean the yard and I am happy."

*

Now that she is back at Al Hummar, Haya no longer has to endure lessons with Mrs Goddard. Santi comes down to the round pen with her each day to help school Bree.

"Bree must accept the bit, and work as a true dressage horse," Santi teaches Haya. "She must respond to the lightest touch."

This is not easy on a horse like Bree. She is willing and so clever, but she is also inexperienced and Haya must teach her everything right from the beginning. Santi shows her how to use her legs to move the filly not only forward, but sideways, and how to tune Bree in to her cues so that she requires only the slightest tap of the heel to change pace, or the softest tightening of

the reins to come back to a halt. Bree can be a little hot-headed. When Haya's signals confuse her, she will toss in an objectionable buck as if to say, "Really, I don't understand what you are asking me to do!"

"You see how she tells you her thoughts?" Santi says when Bree does this. "She is not being naughty, she is talking to you. You must always be clear so she understands what you are asking. It is about developing a language between you. In this way, we school the horse."

Haya's own schooling is looming. The new term at Badminton is about to begin.

"I don't want to go," she tells Zayn.

They are grooming Bree together, and the words tumble out of Haya's mouth before she can stop them.

"Then don't go," Zayn says. "Stay here. Come to my school. You would like it."

Haya sighs. "It's not that simple. My father went to school in England and my Mama too. It has been arranged and I must respect tradition – it is my duty."

She reaches out her hand to stroke Bree's muzzle. The idea of leaving her horse is unbearable.

"Do you wish sometimes that you weren't bound by duty?" Zayn asks.

"What do you mean?"

"You know, do you wish that you were not a Princess?"

Zayn's question takes Haya by surprise. "No!" She shakes her head. "My family are my great strength. My father and mother both taught me what it means to have true love and devotion to my country and its people. Horses are not my escape – I do not need to run away. Horses are my expression. When I am on a horse, I am truly myself. It's my soul in the clear light of day."

Zayn is staring at her now and Haya looks down at her toes, suddenly embarrassed. "I am talking too much. Hand me the pitchfork and I will help you to muck out the boxes."

Bree does not know that Haya is leaving. How could she possibly know? And yet the filly seems to sense that there is something wrong. Each day, when Haya arrives at her loose box, Bree whinnies for her and there is an edge of longing to the cries, as if she knows that each time she sees Haya may be the last.

"I am going away to England tomorrow," Haya tells Zayn, "and I need you to do something for me."

"Of course, Princess Haya. What is it?"

"I need you to look after Bree. I want you to be the one to ride her while I am gone. I want you to be her groom and feed her and care for her and write to me and tell me how she is."

"I'll take good care of her."

"I mean it! This is serious, Zayn, you have to promise me." Haya bites her lip to fight back the tears. "Promise me that you will look after her as if she were your own horse. If anything happens to her…"

"It won't," Zayn says. "I'll keep her safe and care for her until you return, Princess Haya. You have my word."

*

Haya adjusts the stiff collar on her blouse, and wrestles with the knot of her school tie. She is not used to wearing a uniform and the tie feels like it is about to choke her. She reaches down and yanks at her knee socks, which keep slipping and sagging at her ankles.

On the lawn, the girls in their blazers and straw boaters gather in groups, stare and whisper and then act aloof and pretend that they haven't noticed the arrival of the new girl. But how can you fail to see the two giant black limousines with black tinted windows, flying the Union Jack and the royal flag of Jordan?

"Are you ready, Your Royal Highness?" The man sitting beside her in a dark navy suit prepares to open the door while Haya self-consciously fiddles with her tie.

Haya nods nervously and he speaks into his walkie-talkie, communicating to the car in front. "We're going in."

The car door opens and Haya emerges, flanked by two bodyguards; already a third bodyguard is halfway up the footpath waiting for them. Haya walks up the path and tries to smile and to ignore the way the girls stare at her. It was bad enough having her old bodyguard constantly shadowing her at the palace, but now that she is in England the British Government has assigned not one but three agents on rotating security detail to watch over her. So much for fitting in and being a regular girl.

The main building of the school is a stately manor with wisteria vines climbing the stone walls and gigantic pear-shaped topiary standing sentry down the path to the front entrance. It is all very *English*, as is the man in the tweed suit who stands on the steps waiting for her.

"Good morning, Haya." She notices how the headmaster greets her, making a point of not using her royal title, yet she must use his title and address him always as *Mr* Gould.

"Your governess has spoken with us at great length," Mr Gould says. "She insisted that you are a normal girl and must be treated as such."

Was that what Frances actually said? Or was it more along the lines of *Princess Haya is a royal spoilt brat so see that you take her down a peg or two, or you'll have a troublemaker on your hands*? Certainly the headmaster seems to go to great pains, as they stroll round the grounds, to point out the rules and regulations, followed up with a vigorous lecture on curfews and the consequences for those who step outside the grounds without permission. Haya begins to wonder if this is a private school or a prison.

The bodyguards do not help matters and behave as if there might be assassins lurking behind the giant hedges or in the gym lockers. "You will sleep in a dormitory room with twelve other girls," Mr Gould says. "We've provided an additional room in another wing to accommodate your security team."

From the outside Badminton School looks rather grand and austere, but inside Haya is surprised to see that the corridors and classrooms are painted a cheery yellow with blue trim. With all the rules laid out and Haya not showing any signs of dissent, Mr Gould softens a little and makes a few jokes, in Latin, as he shows Haya where she will study sciences, maths and languages. It is not until the tour has almost come to an end and they still haven't laid eyes on any horses that Haya asks, "Can we see the stables, please?"

"Ah," Mr Gould says. "We'd been told that you are a keen equestrienne. I'm sure you will enjoy our weekly lessons here at Badminton."

The stables are right beside the school. Haya is introduced to a rosy-cheeked instructor in a tweed hacking jacket and gets a sinking feeling that this will be Mrs Goddard all over again. As for the ponies themselves, they are such strange creatures! They are solidly built and so round in the belly they make the Tanks look skinny! Some of these ponies are so fat that Haya wonders how she will ever get her legs round them to ride. The ponies are doe-eyed and dozy, the complete opposite to Bree and the leggy, highly strung Arabians back home. They look as foreign as Haya feels in her dormitory, which seems to be filled with long-limbed, blue-eyed blondes.

Haya has never really spent that much time with girls her own age before. Now, in the open-plan dorm room, she is suddenly surrounded by twelve of them. And yet she has never felt more alone in her life. All the other girls seem to know each other already. They sit on their beds and giggle and whisper and braid each other's hair. No one even talks to the Princess.

Haya makes herself busy putting away her things and hanging up her uniform in the closet. She takes dusty old Doll out of her suitcase and props her up on the pillow of her bed, then she unpacks her books and stares out of the window at the green manicured lawns. She thinks of Baba and Ali back home at Al Nadwa palace and wonders what they are doing right now. And, with a pang, she thinks about Bree. She said goodbye to the filly before she left, but Haya knows that Bree will not understand why she doesn't come to see her tomorrow or the next day or the day after that. Bree will think Haya has abandoned her. And that was the last thing Haya ever wanted to do.

Everything is strange at Badminton. In the dining room that evening, Haya asks the cook serving up the food what the dish is called and the woman looks at her as if she were mad. "It's sausages: sausages and mash. What's the matter? Haven't you ever seen a sausage before?"

Haya sits alone and tries not to meet the eyes of the other girls as she eats. She stares at her plate and chokes the strange food down, but she cannot bring herself to eat the sausages and pushes them to one side. She still hates to eat meat. That is the one thing about home that she will definitely not miss – miserable mealtimes with Frances.

Haya's governess knew why she didn't want to eat red meat, but would deliberately serve up great slabs of lamb or chunks of steak on Haya's plate and force her to sit at the table until she ate it. If Haya refused, she would stick it in the fridge and then bring it back out, the same plate every dinnertime, until the meat was so old it was like shoe leather curling up at the edges. Sometimes, after Haya had refused her shrivelled meat one too many times, Frances would send Haya to her room as punishment, not realising that Zuhair or one of the kitchen staff would smuggle food up to Haya in spite of her orders.

Well, Haya thinks, *Frances must be loving it now.* This is what she always wanted – Haya out of sight and out of her way.

After dinner, Baba phones her, just as he said he would, but she is not allowed to speak for long on the dormitory line as it is almost time for lights out. Haya wants to cry down the phone that she hates it here and please, please, can't she be allowed to come back home? But she doesn't of course. She knows that Baba would only be upset and she doesn't want him to worry. Everything is good, she tells him, everything is just fine. Her father hears the note of anxiety in her voice and he tells her that once classes begin she will settle in and make friends. And then Ali is on the other end of the phone and Haya cannot help welling up with tears as he tells her that he misses her.

She is so homesick, for the palace and for Baba and Ali and for Bree. Oh, how much she misses Bree!

She hangs up the phone and goes back to her dorm room. She has never slept in a room with twelve strangers before. And how could anyone sleep when the room is abuzz with conversation? The matron keeps coming in and telling them to be quiet, but as soon as she is gone, they begin to gossip again. It takes ages until the room is quiet at last and all the other girls are asleep. It is well after midnight when the matron does her final check and only then does Haya dare to get out of bed again.

Sitting on the floor beside her bed, Haya tries to be quiet as she works the fastenings on her suitcase and takes her treasure box from inside. Everything is exactly as she left it, and she goes through her familiar routine, working by touch in the darkness of the dorm room, methodically picking up each item and putting it aside as if cataloguing the contents of the box like a museum archivist. There are her mother's sunglasses, the cassette tapes and the stiff dried flowers. When she picks up the braid of coarse black hair that she cut from Bree's tail, she feels her heart aching as if it were going to break in two.

Finally she takes out a grainy black and white photo of her and Mama. It is too dark to see it properly and besides, the tears blur her vision. Haya kisses the photo and then she puts it away again in the box with the rest of the treasures. Then she climbs back into bed and, cuddling Doll in her arms, she cries a little, very softly so that no one can hear her, the tears soaking into her pillow, dampening it beneath her cheek as she goes to sleep.

Chapter 13

The Upper Third at Badminton

As she enters the dining room for breakfast, Haya tries not to meet the eyes of the other boarders. She loads up her tray with scrambled eggs and toast and finds an unoccupied table. She feels self-conscious sitting alone, but she is too shy to try and join the others so she is trying to act oblivious to her surroundings and focus hard on her food. This is why it takes her a few seconds to notice that there is a girl standing beside her.

"You shouldn't eat that."

Haya looks up. It is one of the blondes from her dormitory.

"I'm sorry?" Haya says.

The blonde casts a knowing glance back over at

her friends at the other table. There are four of them, cloistered together giggling, and they all have their eyes fixed on Haya's table.

"The eggs, I mean," the blonde says. "It's a new girl thing. You'll learn once you've been here for a while. Never get the scrambled eggs – they taste like old socks. The trick is to sidestep the eggs and get two servings of sausages. The cooks tell you off, but just ignore them and smile and take an extra piece of toast too."

The blonde girl plonks herself down at the table beside Haya. "My name is Claire Booth," she says. "Do I have to call you Your Majesty?"

"My father is Your Majesty," Haya says. "I am Princess Haya."

"That is so cool!" Claire Booth says. "Princess Haya." She says it to see how the words feel coming out of her mouth and then she looks back over her shoulder and pulls a face at her friends who are watching her, wide-eyed in disbelief.

"*They* were all too scared to come and talk to you," she says. "*They* think you're going to be stuck-up because you are a princess, but you're not, are you?"

Haya frowns. She doesn't know what the word means, but she assumes it isn't good.

"Do you live in a palace?" Claire asks.

"Yes," Haya says, "but it's just like a house really."

"I bet it's huge!" Claire says. "Do you have lots of servants? We have a housekeeper twice a week at home and I had a nanny when I was little, of course, and there's a gardener who comes sometimes, but we don't have butlers or anything really posh like that. My dad's a surgeon. We're not filthy rich or anything. Not like some of the girls here. Does your dad have loads of oil wells?"

Haya shakes her head. "There is no oil in Jordan."

"Well, diamond mines then!" Claire Booth says briskly, clearly not wanting factual details to get in the way of a good story. She looks up at the bodyguard who is standing at the door of the dining hall and watching her warily. She gives him a cheery wave. "Do you have bodyguards with you all the time? What do they do when you go to the bathroom? I suppose they wait outside. Are they going to come to school with you each day? Can you get them to do your homework for you?"

"My father makes me have them," Haya says. She has never met someone who can talk so fast! "Back home in Jordan my brother and I are always running away from them."

"I wish I was a princess," Claire sighs. "I bet your

whole life is super-glamorous and you jet-set about and hang out with gorgeous princes who buy you gifts and go on luxury yachts, and you've probably already met loads of celebrities at those fabulous parties in the south of France!"

Haya shakes her head in disbelief. "No, I haven't."

"Well, do you wear a tiara when you're at home?"

"No!" Haya giggles at the idea of wandering around the stables at Al Hummar dressed in a tiara.

"Ohhh! If I had a crown, I'd wear it all the time!" Claire says excitedly. "Only I don't think my hair would be right with a crown. I'm thinking of getting it cut because it's too curly and it never looks any good. I wish I had hair like you! Where do you get yours cut? My mum takes me into London and we have this hairdresser in Knightsbridge who does absolutely everyone's hair..."

Claire sits with Haya for lunch that day too, and at dinnertime she asks Haya to sit at her table with her friends. The friends don't talk as much as Claire does, but they seem mostly nice. All of them want to hear stories about life in Arabia, except for the tall blonde with a short bob and ski-slope nose called Stephanie, who looks extremely bored. Stephanie hardly ever smiles and she looks Haya up and down in the way that Frances used to do.

When they are leaving the dinner table that night to go back to their dorm rooms, Haya is walking across the quad alone when she sees Stephanie directly ahead of her.

"Oh, yah," Stephanie is saying to the girl walking with her. "We had dinner with her. She's a *real* princess. Totally arrogant, like she just goes on about herself all the time, talking about how she wants to ride horses, but the ones here are all too fat – not good enough for *her*." And then, in a low whisper, she adds, "My father says they're all like that. Middle Eastern royalty. They're so used to being given everything that they think they can just snap their fingers and everyone will fall over themselves because they have so much money. Her daddy, the King, donated a new library to the school apparently. That's how she got in…"

Haya feels her face flushing hot. It isn't true! And she only meant that the horses here weren't like the ones back home! She wants to run up and tell Stephanie then and there, but it would do no good. She hurries back across the lawn, trying to hide the tears that are welling in her eyes.

Homesickness, Haya is beginning to realise, is a lot like grief. It is always with you, but if you want to have any happiness, then you must call a truce of sorts with your heart and get on with life. She had thought that the stables would be her sanctuary here at boarding school, but the smell and the sound of the horses make her long for Al Hummar. And the way they ride, doing nothing but boring quadrilles in the arena, is no fun at all. She needs to take her mind off horses and try something new.

"Have you ever played hockey?" Claire asks her. "There are try-outs next week. I'm going – you should come along."

"As long as we can be on the same team," Haya says. "I wouldn't like to confront you with a stick, you'd be deadly."

"Oh, I'm usually too busy talking to hit anything," Claire says blithely.

It is Haya who turns out to be the deadly one. She is a natural athlete, and is soon Badminton's star hockey player. She is good at netball too, and tennis, swimming and gymnastics. If she has to be here at boarding school, then she is determined to do her very best and make her father proud.

"You're such a swot. You always get A's in absolutely everything," Claire sighs.

"I got a B in maths," Haya objects. "And I'm going

to get thrown out of choir if they catch us talking again."

"I wish they'd throw us both out!" Claire says. "Anyway, it's their fault for making it so dull. If I didn't talk to you, I'd fall asleep."

The blondes that Haya once found so daunting are now her friends. Even the problem with Stephanie vanishes after the Upper Third's class trip to London. It is supposed to be a geography trip, but really it is more like a day of sightseeing. In the afternoon, the girls visit Buckingham Palace and as they stand outside the gates Haya cannot resist leaning over to Stephanie and whispering, "My daddy is buying me this place; we're going to demolish all the buildings and turn the gardens into fields for my horses."

Stephanie's eyes widen and her mouth hangs open in horror. Haya manages to keep a straight face and look serious for a second, before losing it and bursting into fits of giggles. It is a risky joke, but when Stephanie begins laughing too, Haya knows that the coldness between them is over.

Baba and Ali write to Haya every day, although Ali's letters always say exactly the same thing. He is counting down until the end of term even though Haya has only just arrived.

Dear Haya,

53 days until you come home
I love u

Ali

Dear Haya
52 days until you come home
I love u
Ali

Mondays are the best because the letters have been saved up from the weekend and so Haya often gets three from Baba and three from Ali. One Monday morning, however, there is an extra letter, written in a hand she does not recognise. She opens the envelope and begins to scan the lines of scrawly writing and quickly realises it is from Zayn.

Your Royal Highness, Princess Haya,

I hope things are good at your new school. I know that I promised you that I would write with news, but I'm really not very good at writing. I hope you can read the words and I'm sorry if I make mistakes.

Bint Al-Reeh hasn't been so good since you left. At first, when she stopped eating, we thought she had a virus. But the vet says she's perfectly healthy. The filly stands at her door night and day and whinnies and Yusef says she is pining. Santi says it is because of her Arab blood – it makes a horse loyal. And Bree is a true Arabian, devoted to only one master – you.

I had to tell you because I promised I would write, but please don't worry. Bree has started to eat now and I feed her by hand every day to make sure. I am writing this letter sitting on the straw in her loose box and when I told her just now that I was writing to you she seemed to cheer up. She even sniffed the letter with her muzzle – so I suppose she's signed it with a kiss. She is waiting for the day when you will return, Inshallah. Until then, may Allah keep you safe and well.

Your faithful servant (and friend),

Zayn

In the dining hall, Haya's hands tremble as she reads the letter. All this time she had been missing Bree so much, it never occurred to her that the filly would miss her too. She wishes desperately, more than anything, that she was home.

She folds the letter from Zayn and puts it in the breast pocket of her blazer, takes a deep breath and pulls herself together. There is no time for sorrow. It is 8.30 and she is late for maths.

In class, though, she cannot focus on the questions in her exercise book. All she can think about is Bree. She feels so helpless, being stuck here. She gives up on the maths problems and begins to write. She uses the back pages of her book, scribbling furiously, and by the time the class is over she has composed a letter back to Zayn, telling him all the things she knows about Bree. She tells him all her secrets – like the way the filly loves being scratched on her rump. *Don't be afraid when you start scratching and she reverses her hindquarters at you as if she is trying to take aim to kick you,* Haya writes, *it just means she wants you to scratch her tail. Oh – and for a treat if it is hot she loves ice cream – she licks it from the cone very daintily like a lady – oh, and she adores peppermints! I have taught her to nod her head and ask before I give her one. Also, if she is pacing in her box, maybe she is bored? Take her on a forest ride and let her gallop. I only got the chance to do this a few times before I went away, but it was the best. Bree loves to gallop…*

For the next week Haya checks the postbox compulsively, desperate for news. When a letter from Zayn finally arrives, Haya tears at the envelope, her heart racing. As she begins to read, her eyes prick with tears, not of sorrow, but joy. *I have done everything you told me in your letter*, Zayn writes. *When I took her to the forest, she was fretting at the bit so I let her have her head and gallop just as you told me and we must have gone for three miles before she tired enough to slow back down to a trot. She was a different horse on the ride home and from that moment her spirits lifted. You can imagine how happy I was when she ate all of her feed when we got home.*

Haya still misses Bree, but it is good to know that the filly is no longer pining. Haya's own homesickness too begins to abate, but she still dreams of being back in Jordan, galloping on her horse through the forests. If only she could ride like that in England! There is little hope of finding kindred spirits here when it comes to horses. Or at least that is what she thinks.

Chapter 14

Challenger

My dearest Baba,

It is hard to believe that it's already the second term. I wish I could have come home for the holidays instead of staying at school for the hockey tournament. We had our first classes of the new term today and I got my exam results back. I got 89 per cent in English and I got A's in all of my subjects, yes, even maths, so tell that to Frances!

It is cold in England – and it rains all the time. The horses here wear heavy rugs and they clip them, shaving all their hair off with shears and cutting patterns in the fur, leaving bits of coat on the top to keep their backs warm. It looks very odd.

The riding school ponies are lazy and you have to kick them and kick them to make them go. No wonder they are so slow when all the instructors let you do is ride round the arena doing quadrilles. We are hardly ever allowed to do any jumping!! It sounds mad, but I am thinking of giving up riding entirely for the rest of the year – did I tell you they have made me captain of the school hockey team?

Oh – also I have exciting news for Ali. One of the girls here has a father who does something to do with football for Manchester United and when Ali comes to England to visit me next term she has promised that we can go and meet the players and watch a game. Tell Ali that I miss him. I cannot wait to come home. I miss everyone so much. I love you very much, Baba.

Your daughter, Haya

*

On Sundays the Badminton pupils are allowed to take the ponies out of the arena and go hacking in the country lanes surrounding the school. The girls use this outing as an excuse to get out of school without supervision and head for the village shops. Haya often sees their poor horses, bored rigid, tied up to the hitching rail by the village green while the girls giggle and flirt with the boys from the nearby local school.

On one of these Sunday afternoons Haya is hacking along the lane on Tempest, a brown Fell pony gelding that the instructors at Badminton describe as bombproof and Haya would describe as half dead. She is thinking how it will take her forever to reach the village at this rate when she looks up and sees two riders moving at a flat gallop over the nearby field.

The rider at the front sits astride a heavy-boned bay hunter and rides boldly, urging the horse on the way Haya has seen racing jockeys do. Right behind her is another rider on an elegant, showy chestnut. It is too far away for Haya to see the riders clearly, but they certainly look very experienced. Haya watches as they approach a five-barred gate that leads from one field to the next and is surprised when they do not slow down in the slightest. She realises with shock that they are going to jump it! The big bay hunter goes first and the chestnut follows, both horses taking the jump off lovely forward strides, then continuing at a gallop without breaking pace.

"Why can't we do that?" she murmurs to Tempest as she gives him a slappy pat on his rugged brown neck.

In the village, Haya is coming out of the sweet shop when she hears the staccato chink of metal shoes on the tarmac. She turns to see the chestnut and the bay that were jumping the fences between fields turning the corner of the lane. The riders she thought were adult professionals turn out to be girls the same age as Haya! She is certain she's never seen them at Badminton. Their horses are sweaty and blowing still from the gallop, and the girls' reins are hanging loose as they ride and chat. They look as if they are heading towards the café by the village green and without thinking Haya seizes her chance and runs across to meet them.

"Hello," she says, panting a little as she catches up.

The girl on the big bay is very pretty with long blonde hair tied back in a thick plait. She pulls the bay to a halt. "Hello," she smiles warmly. She looks at Haya's helmet and jodhpurs and then back over at Tempest, who is tied to the hitching rail by the green. "Is he your pony?"

"No," Haya says. "Well, yes, but he's not mine. He belongs to the school."

"Oh," the girl says. "Are you at Badminton?"

"Yes, that's right," Haya says. She is losing her nerve a little, but she takes a deep breath. "I saw you riding through the fields on my way here. I love jumping. We never jump at our school, well, hardly ever. And the ponies aren't up to much."

"You should come and have lessons with us," the blonde girl says. "We go to Shepperlands Copse. It's not far from here. Lucinda and I have our own horses stabled there, but the Ramsays, they're the ones who run the place, they have some really decent school horses too – if you want to do real riding, I mean."

Haya tries to contain her excitement and not just shout, "Yes, please – take me with you!" She is certain for some reason that she has heard the name Ramsay before back in Jordan too.

"My name is Jemima," the blonde girl says, "and this is Lucinda..."

Lucinda, however, doesn't say hello. She is distracted by the man in dark glasses loitering beside Tempest.

"Did you realise that there's a chap over there by your pony acting very strangely?" Lucinda says. "Is he one of your teachers?"

"No," Haya sighs. "He's my bodyguard."

*

On the ride home Haya's excitement at her chance encounter starts to dwindle. Badminton School may not be so enthusiastic about her traipsing off across to Shepperlands Copse for lessons when their own riding school is in the grounds. How is she going to convince

them to let her go?

Haya is still mulling this over the next morning at breakfast when the post arrives. There is a letter from Baba. She reads the first few paragraphs with great interest, as her father writes about life at home at Al Nadwa. But it is when she reaches the fourth paragraph that Haya's eyes widen in surprise.

I have spoken to Santi after your last letter, her father writes, *and he reminded me that he has old acquaintances from England who once visited us here in Jordan. Their name is Ramsay – Richard and Marjorie Ramsay. They run a very professional stable that sounds perfect for you. Santi has contacted them and it has been arranged with the school that you may be given leave for lessons after school and on weekends. The name of the stables is Shepperlands Copse and it is very near your school...*

Haya cannot believe her eyes. It is the same place that the girls in the village told her about!

The next weekend Haya pulls on her jodhpurs and her bodyguard drives her over to Shepperlands Copse yard. Richard Ramsay is in the middle of giving a lesson when she arrives and so Haya waits for him in his office. She is admiring the champion sashes from the Horse of the

Year, the Royal Windsor Show and Olympia, strung up all over the walls, when she hears hoofbeats in the stable corridor and familiar voices.

"Oh, hello again!" Jemima says with delight when Haya emerges from the office. "Mr Ramsay said we would have a new girl joining our ride, but I had no idea it would be you!"

Behind her comes a tall, smartly kitted-out man in beige breeches and a khaki gilet leading a grey pony. "You girls have already met?" Mr Ramsay is surprised. "Well, that makes life easier. We can dispense with the introductions and get started then."

The grey pony that Mr Ramsay is leading is called Toby and he is intended for Haya. "He's a real showjumping schoolmaster," Mr Ramsay tells her as they head for the arena.

"Hello, Toby." Haya takes the reins and looks the grey gelding in the eye. There is a kindness about this pony, but a feisty spirit in there too. She likes him immediately.

The Ramsays' arena is set up with showjumps and painted rails arranged in a course just like on TV at the Horse of the Year Show with pot plants at the corners and everything. Haya's only other jumping experience has been over jumps that she made herself on the Tank. Not that she is about to tell Jemima and Lucinda that. They are both so elegant, mounted up on entirely different ponies to the ones that Haya saw them exercising earlier in the week, looking every bit as confident on showjumpers in the arena as they did on hunters out in the fields.

"Take your stirrups up to jumping length," says Mr Ramsay. Haya didn't even know there was such a thing as jumping length, but she takes the stirrups up a couple of holes and joins in at the back of the ride behind Lucinda. It is hard enough to keep up at a trot with these two riders, and when Mr Ramsay calls out instructions to the girls, it is like he is speaking another language. "Your pony is too much on the forehand, Jemima; give him a half-halt! Better. Make him use his hindquarters more, Lucinda. More leg and less hand! Good…"

The first fifteen minutes of the lesson they do not jump at all; they trot and canter and work on their position in the saddle. Mr Ramsay shows Haya how to ride perched up on her stirrups in two-point position. Then he shows her how to make a bridge with her reins over Toby's neck to help keep her hands in a crest release so that she won't jag Toby in the mouth as they go over the fences.

"Right then!" he says brightly. "You're looking quite secure up there – you've clearly got natural balance. Why don't you follow behind the others and pop over the red and white rails, then the blue and white planks, and let's see how we go?"

As Jemima and Lucinda confidently steam off ahead on their horses, Haya does her best to keep up. Toby leaps off from too far back on both fences and she is quite certain Mr Ramsay must be able to see blue sky between her legs and the saddle as she gets left behind both times, but she manages to stay onboard. Thankfully Mr Ramsay doesn't chastise her like Mrs Goddard would surely have done.

"I like the way you let Toby have his head and kept the release even though you were left behind," he says. "You've got good hands. We just need to work on those legs of yours."

As Mr Ramsay walks round the jumping course lowering the fences to cross rails, he talks to the girls about the importance of the lower leg. "It must never leave the horse's side at any stage when they are jumping. That is where your security comes from. Position your lower leg, plug in those seat bones and sit up.

"Right!" he says as he lowers the last jump in the course. "Can we have you on your own this time, please, Princess Haya?"

When Haya finishes jumping the small crossbars, Mr Ramsay raises them back up to their original height for the other girls and Haya watches on the sidelines as Jemima and Lucinda take their turn over the bigger jumps. She watches the way they canter in with perfect timings and flying changes at the jumps and she is aware of just how good these girls are, and even more aware that she is not as good as them. *Not yet anyway*. Watching the other girls, she is gripped by a desire to rise to their level.

If Jemima and Lucinda realise that they are better riders than Haya, they don't gloat about it. After lessons, the three of them hang back at the stables to help the Ramsays muck out and feed.

"What are the Arabians like at the Royal Stables?" Jemima wants to know. "I bet they're gorgeous!" Haya finds herself telling them all about Bree, and the stables at Al Hummar.

Being a part of the team at the Ramsays' encourages Haya to raise her game. Her ability comes on in leaps and bounds and soon she is riding the same fences as Jemima and Lucinda. She is discovering that showjumping is not just about pointing the horse at the fences, being brave and hoping for the best. She is learning how to ride in deep to a fence and judge the stride so that the horse takes off at the perfect moment.

When Haya started, she thought that a cavaletti was huge. Now the jumps go up to eighty centimetres, then a metre, and a metre ten. When they reach a metre twenty, Mr Ramsay pronounces them, "Too big for Toby." He tries her on several of his jumpers before eventually settling for Victorious, a headstrong, A-grade competition pony. Haya clicks with Victorious immediately. The jumps go higher still.

*

One day when Haya arrives at the yard, Jemima greets her waving a piece of paper in her hand. "We've been entered," she tells her. "There's a local showjumping tournament on this weekend. You're riding Victorious in three classes!"

It's just a country show, but to Haya it might as well be the Grand Prix at Olympia. She is so nervous the night before she spends an hour unable to sleep, rearranging the contents of her treasure box. She is about to put it away, but then she changes her mind and opens the lid again, taking out the braid of hair that she cut from Bree's tail. "You'll be my good-luck charm tomorrow," she whispers as she slips the braid into the pocket of her show jacket.

Jemima and Lucinda have ridden loads of competitions before and their cheerful ease as they prepare the ponies helps Haya to relax too. They load the ponies into the Ramsays' horse lorry and then all three girls pile in the back as they head off for the competition.

By the time they arrive at 7am, there are already riders in the showjumping arena walking the course. They are jumping a metre ten today in the show ring, which is not as big as they have been practising at the stables. All the same, as she stands next to the fences, which come up to her chest, Haya feels her stomach tie in a knot. There is one set of coloured rails that Mr Ramsay refers to as a 'rider frightener' because it is so wide and imposing.

"If you ask me, it's the double that's going to cause the problems. You'll need to put in a really big stride or you'll take out the back rails," Jemima says as she strides out the distances between the fences with the other girls.

Haya stands in the middle of the course and traces a track in the air with her finger, figuring out which order to take the jumps in. She hopes she remembers which ones she is meant to jump – it would be awful to be disqualified for an error.

In the warm-up ring, she waits and watches while the other riders take their turns. Jemima and Lucinda are both up before her and they do well, but the white gate and the coloured rails both prove tricky and the girls have four faults apiece.

Just before she is about to go into the ring, Haya rides Victorious twice over the practice jump. The gelding pops over the rails so neatly she feels a surge of confidence. When she hears her name being called and enters the ring, she forgets to be nervous and suddenly all her focus is on the fences.

As soon as the bell rings, she is through the flags at a bold canter, taking the first jump with determination just as Mr Ramsay taught her to do. Victorious gets a little strong at the second fence and she checks him before driving him on, and they are over jump number two with air to spare. Haya had been so worried that she would forget the course, but now that she is out there riding, the adrenaline is flowing. She remembers it so clearly that in midair over each jump she is already turning her pony, preparing it for the next fence. Victorious fights her coming into the double and Haya has to trust the gelding to get his own striding right as she lets go of him and kicks on. Luckily Victorious is a smart horse and even though he takes off too far back he manages to make up with a big stride in the middle. Then Haya is pulling hard

on the reins and setting him up for the last fence, which the pony flies with ease. They are clear!

From their three events Haya and Victorious win three prizes – a first and two thirds. Haya has to stop herself from taking the ribbons out and admiring them all the way home. Jemima and Lucinda also come home with prize ribbons from their events and back at the stables the girls tie their sashes round their horses' necks and take photos. Haya gives Victorious a hug as she puts him away in his loose box with extra feed.

"Ohh, let me see!" Claire Booth grabs the prize ribbons off her when she gets back to the boarding house that evening.

"I like the yellow ones the best," Claire says. "I'd try to win them."

"But the red one is first place," Haya tries to explain. "That is like wanting a bronze medal instead of gold."

"I don't care," Claire insists. "The yellow ones are prettiest."

In her room, Haya considers putting the ribbons away in her treasure box, but then changes her mind and strings them up over her bed between the posters that she has ripped out of magazines.

*

Showjumping and schoolwork often clash and Haya has to spend her evenings working on a history essay or a maths assignment until late at night so that she can keep up with her schoolwork. Yet, despite spending so much time at the Ramsays' yard, she feels more and more a part of school life too. Most evenings after she has done her homework, she hangs out in the dormitory common room with the other girls from the Upper Third.

The headmaster insists that they watch the news each night, not just music shows, because it is important to know about world events. Haya watches images of fighting in the Persian Gulf and listens as the BBC journalist talks in serious tones about the war. She feels the distance between England and Arabia more than ever. And although she has settled in, she misses Baba and Ali and Bree every single day. The treasure box remains in the top drawer of the chest by her bed, and every night she opens it to look at the black and white photo of her Mama. She never forgets that this is a strange land and she is a very long way from home.

"Are you going to watch the space shuttle?" Claire asks Haya one afternoon when they are on their way back to the dorms.

Everyone in the dorm is going to watch the Challenger

take-off. The newspapers have been filled with little else for the past few weeks. This is not the first shuttle that NASA has sent into space, but it is the first time that ordinary men and women are joining the astronauts on the trip. Haya has watched them being interviewed and she thinks that one of the astronauts, a woman with long dark hair, looks a lot like her old nanny, Grace.

In the common room, the girls gather round the TV. Haya and Claire both lie down on the floor, propped up on cushions right in front of the screen.

"Keep your heads down," someone at the back insists. "We can't see the screen."

The astronauts are walking in their spacesuits, helmets tucked under their arms, as they leave the media conference and prepare to board the space shuttle. The news cameras cut to the grandstand at Kennedy Space Center in Florida. It is a cold day and the watching crowds are dressed up warmly in jumpers, scarves and coats. They have binoculars in their hands and their expectant faces are locked on the shuttle, which is perched on top of the big rocket boosters. There is excitement in the air and the crowds cheer when the astronauts emerge to take the walk along the ramp, giving a final wave as they board the shuttle. They are ready for take-off.

On the floor of the common room Haya rests her chin on her pillow and watches as the rockets power up and white steam begins to come out all around the launch pad.

"*T-minus twenty-one seconds and the solid rocket booster engine is now under way…*" the voice on the TV broadcast crackles. "*Ten-nine-eight-seven-six – we have main engine start – four-three-two-one and lift off! LIFT OFF! The twenty-fifth space shuttle mission has cleared the tower!*"

The crowds in the grandstands shield their eyes as the rocket thrusts up into the cold, clear blue sky. In the common room at Badminton there is a cheer from the girls crowded round the TV.

"That is so awesome!" Claire says as the white streak of cloud marks a track across the sky. "I wish I was going up into space!"

On the TV the astronauts are talking to mission control: "*Engines beginning throttling down now… altitude is 4.3 nautical miles…*"

And then, on the screen, the smooth white cloud trail that has been arcing across the sky suddenly blows apart, exploding in a ball of vapour. It is as if the cloud itself has shattered, shooting off strands of white plume

in every direction. Sparks fly out from the clouds and then an eerie jet stream can be seen, the tail of a glowing fireball plummeting to the earth below.

The voice on the TV is reassuring: "*Looks like a couple of the solid rocket boosters blew away from the side of the shuttle...*"

The cheers in the common room hush. It didn't look like booster rockets. Even though the voice on the TV is calm, it is clear that something is very wrong.

Then a second voice can be heard, this time from NASA control: "*This is obviously a major malfunction.*"

Haya is struggling to make sense of what she is seeing. On the screen the crowds in the grandstand at the Kennedy Space Center are straining their eyes at the sky in stunned confusion and devastated silence. In front of the eyes of the world, the rocket has just exploded in mid-flight. The shuttle, which was supposed to take seven men and women to the outer limits of the atmosphere, has taken them instead on a fiery plunge nine nautical miles to the earth below.

In the common room, the girls of Badminton's Upper Third stare at the TV in disbelief as the camera returns to the sky where the cloud vapour of the explosion still hangs in the air. But on the floor of the common room

Claire is not looking at the TV any more.

"Haya?" Claire stares at her friend. "Haya, what is it? Are you OK?"

Grief is a living thing. It bides its time, holding your heart in its dark hand, and waits for its moment to give a squeeze. For eight years grief has cradled Haya's heart. Now it tightens its fist. From a thousand miles away she watches the rocket fall from the sky and, as it falls, she sees her mother's face, the lightning strike and then the screaming terror as the helicopter plummets to earth.

"Haya?"

The girls crowd round her.

"What's wrong with her?"

"Get back and give her some air!" someone says.

Haya is crumpled in a ball on the floor, sobs wracking her body, breath coming in short brutal gasps. Grief is choking her, tightening its grip. This time it has no intention of letting go.

CHAPTER 15

Home

Haya feels so exhausted, the room is swimming in front of her and she cannot think straight. She is in her room at the dormitory and her father is here with her, beside her bed, stroking her hair.

"Baba," she sobs softly. "I'm so sorry…"

"Shhh!" the King says. "Don't worry, Haya. Everything is going to be OK. I'm taking you home…"

At the airport the black state cars flying the red, white, black and green colours of the Jordanian flag cruise across the runway to meet the royal jet.

"I don't want to fly," Haya murmurs as her father carries her onboard the plane, but the doctor has given her some pills that keep her calm. She barely remembers the flight home. At one point, she looks out of the window at the blue Mediterranean Sea stretching out below and she thinks about falling down out of the sky. She clutches Doll in her arms and gazes sleepily out of the window, feeling numb.

When she wakes again, her father is beside her bed once more, and she is home. They are back at Al Nadwa palace. She feels like Dorothy from *The Wizard of Oz* waking up in Kansas.

"You need to rest," her father says. "Sleep some more. Tomorrow you will feel much better."

The next day Haya wakes up with a sore head and a thumping noise echoing in her ears. *Bang, bang, bang*. It is Ali kicking a football against the wall in her bedroom.

"What are you doing?" Haya groans.

"You're awake!" Ali grins. Then he adds, "You look terrible."

"Thanks."

"You've been asleep for ages. Baba has gone to the Royal Court. He left half an hour ago. Frances said I had to stay away and let you sleep." Ali picks up the football. "Do you want to play on my Scaletrix set? You can pick any car you want – I've got the silver one though…"

"Prince Ali!"

It is Frances, standing in the doorway of Haya's bedroom.

"You were supposed to leave the Princess to sleep," Frances says, bustling into the room and shooing Ali away from Haya's bedside.

"No," Haya says, swinging her legs over the side of the bed. "It's OK, Frances. I was going to get up anyway. I want to go to the stables."

"Out of the question," Frances says briskly. "The doctor told me you should spend the day in bed."

"I'm not going to just lie here all day," Haya says. "I have to see Bree."

"The doctor says you need to rest." Frances lifts Haya's legs back into the bed and vigorously tucks the blankets in around her.

"Then I want to talk to the doctor myself…" Haya says.

"Don't be ridiculous!" Frances says.

"…or I will phone my father at the Royal Court and talk to him about it." Haya has made it all the way home to Bree and she is not about to be held prisoner in her own bed by her governess.

By the time the doctor arrives Haya has had a shower and eaten breakfast and is already dressed in her jodhpurs.

"The Princess tells me that she is feeling much better. A short trip to the stables should be fine," the doctor tells Frances. "The fresh air will be good for her."

Haya waits until Frances and the doctor both leave her room before she collapses back on to the bed again. The whole time they were here she was worried that she might faint. She has to grip the railing to steady herself as she walks down the staircase, but she is determined not to let Frances know how feeble she is. Nothing is going to stop her from seeing Bree.

*

"Titch!" Santi is delighted when Haya turns up in his office. "I heard that you were home, but I did not think you were coming to see us today!"

Haya gives Santi a wan smile. In the car on the way here, she felt a little better, as if the fog that had filled her head for the past few days was beginning to lift, but she still feels weak. "How is Bree?" she asks.

"Come and see for yourself," Santi says. He looks at his watch. "Zayn should have let her out in the exercise yard to stretch her legs. Give me just a moment to organise myself and I will come with you…"

Santi has risen from his chair and they are about to leave when a man in jodhpurs and a khaki shirt strides in through the office door. The man does not knock, but walks straight in. Reacting swiftly, Haya's bodyguard leaps to his feet and steps forward to block his path.

"Whoa!" The man halts in his tracks, a flicker of amusement on his face as he raises his hands in surrender. "What's this, Santi? You have your own guard now? I had no idea you were such an important man!"

Santi gestures to the bodyguard to stand down. "He is with the Princess," he says.

The man turns to Haya. "My apologies, Your Royal Highness, I did not realise you were here. I am Colonel Bashir, head of the Royal Mounted Police and gracious servant of His Majesty King Hussein."

"I know," Haya says, "I have seen you ride. You are very good."

She has seen the colonel compete many times in the King's Cup against the Al Hummar Royal Stables. The Royal Mounted Police are famous for their long string of victories in the hallowed event. In all the years that Haya has been watching the King's Cup, she has never known Bashir to lose.

Bashir beams with pride at Haya's compliment. "I do hope Your Royal Highness will be coming to watch us win the King's Cup again this year?" he says to Haya. "It will be the eleventh consecutive victory for my team."

"Tenth!" Santi scowls at him.

Bashir smiles. "Tenth, is it? Well, who is counting, eh?"

Santi is flustered as he grabs the office keys off his desk. "We were just leaving," he tells Bashir. "Let us see you out on our way."

Haya knows that Santi is unhappy about losing so many times to Bashir. She also knows that he is not the only one. Every year she has sat beside her father in the Royal Box and seen the disappointment on the King's face when Bashir and his team win. Her father is always gracious of course. He makes the speech in their honour every year and runs the red and gold flag of the Mounted Police up the flagpole beside the Royal Box. But Haya can sense his unhappiness every time.

One year, after the cup had been handed once more to Bashir's team, Haya asked her father why it mattered so much to him. After all, both teams were in the service of the Kingdom and both teams rode in his honour. Her father turned to his children and smiled enigmatically. "Even Kings and Queens secretly have their favourite teams."

"It's true, Haya!" Ali had piped up in agreement. "I

heard a rumour that Queen Elizabeth supports Arsenal!"

Haya thinks that her father's passion for Al Hummar is surely its horses. The Arabians of the Royal Stables possess true Bedouin breeding, dating back centuries to the mares of Al Khamseh. These horses are a living embodiment of the heritage of Jordan and her father has fought hard to continue their sacred bloodlines. It is his love of these horses that makes him desire Al Hummar's return to glory. Also, Bashir is kind of annoying. Who wouldn't want to beat him?

"I'm here to discuss the details for this year's cup," Bashir says, brandishing a folder full of paperwork.

"It will have to wait for another time, Bashir," Santi says. "I am taking the Princess to see her horse. Come back and talk to me later."

"Your Royal Highness has a pony?" Bashir smiles. "How nice!"

"It is my dream to ride in the King's Cup one day," Haya says. It has taken courage to admit this to such a rider as Bashir, but when she sees the expression on the man's face, she wishes she had kept quiet.

"Horses are a man's sport," Bashir says, frowning. "Girls do not ride in the cup and in my opinion well-bred ladies should not ride at all."

"Princess Haya is a very good rider, Bashir," Santi says. "And you would be wise not to insult her in my presence again."

Colonel Bashir looks taken aback. "I meant no insult," he insists. "I shall look forward to seeing Your Royal Highness at the cup this year in the Royal Box. In fact, when we win, we shall dedicate our victory to you!"

"You haven't won it yet you know, Bashir," Santi snaps. "Anyway, whatever business you have with me will have to wait. I am busy."

*

The stables at Al Hummar look smaller than they did when Haya left. As she walks through the courtyard, the horses hear her footsteps and crane their necks over the stable doors to say hello. Normally Haya would not be able to pass them by without stopping to give them a pat or feed them a treat, but today there is only one horse she is here to see.

The exercise yard is a bare earth pen on the far side of the building and at first, as Haya comes round the corner, it appears that it is empty. And then, at the far end of the yard, beneath the shade of a solitary tree, she sees the bay filly.

"Bree?"

At the sound of Haya's voice the horse turns her head, ears pricked.

"Bree!"

The whinny cuts through the morning air as she calls back to Haya. Then Bree breaks into a trot as Haya begins to run too, racing across the courtyard and climbing through the rails of the fence to meet her horse.

Bree is in full flight, cantering so fast it looks as if she will mow Haya down! They are about to collide when the horse pulls up hard on her hocks and skids to a stop, dust flying from beneath her feet. She holds her head high and the air is punctuated with her frantic whinnies.

Without a thought for what she is doing, Haya flings herself at her horse, her arms encircling Bree's neck, hugging her as hard as she can. All the while Bree is stamping and nickering. She begins thrusting her muzzle playfully against Haya's chest, as if she is berating her for her absence these long months. "Where have you been?" her nickers seem to say. "I was so worried!"

Haya buries her face in Bree's mane to hide her tears. She does not want Santi to see that she is crying, but she cannot help herself. They are not tears of sorrow, but joy and relief at their reunion. She is home at last.

For a long time she stands there, hugging tight to Bree,

inhaling the sweet, horsey smell of her. When Haya steps back at last, she takes a critical look at the bay horse. "You've got skinny," she says. "You should see the fat ponies where I've just been. It would take two of you to make one of them."

All the same, Bree still looks to be in fair health with a shiny, rich red bay coat and lush black mane and tail. The proportions of her body have caught up to those long lanky legs and, despite the lack of weight, it is clear that in the months that Haya has been gone, Bree has ceased to be a filly and is now a fully grown mare.

Haya tries to move around Bree, to get a good look at her, but it is not easy. Bree will not stand still. She keeps following Haya, nudging and poking her with her muzzle, as if she is unwilling to let her out of her sight, even for a second.

"You're back!" It is Zayn. He drops the bucket of feed and runs to greet her.

"Welcome home, Your Royal Highness," he says. "It's good to see you again."

Haya smiles. "It is good to see you again, Zayn. Thank you for taking such good care of Bree."

"She is a little light, I know," Zayn says. "But now you are here she will soon gain weight."

Bree shoves her nose firmly into Haya as if to confirm this and Haya giggles. "Do you want your feed now then?" she asks the mare.

"Oh," Zayn says. "You don't want to ride her? I have her tack all ready for you."

"I am not sure if the Princess is ready to ride yet," Santi says, looking worried.

"We can go to the forest," Zayn says. "I'll come with you if you want?"

Haya nods weakly. "OK."

Zayn grins. "We can take the new trail; there's a really nice gallop track on it."

A gallop seems like a lofty ambition for a girl who can hardly walk. Haya is so light-headed and weak; her hands shake uncontrollably as she lifts the saddle off the railing.

"Here, let me help you with that." She feels the strong hands of Yusef take the saddle from her and throw it over Bree's back.

"Thank you, Yusef," Haya says.

"You are home now then? School is finished?" Yusef asks her.

"I'm home," Haya confirms. She doesn't mention that school actually has another three weeks before the end of term. It is at least two months before Haya will return to Badminton, if she returns at all.

"I saw that sly one Bashir talking to Santi earlier." Yusef tightens the girth. "What did he want?"

"He came to discuss the King's Cup," Haya says. Then she adds, "I don't think Santi likes him very much."

"Hah!" Yusef grunts in agreement. "That colonel, he is very full of his own importance. He drives Santi mad."

"He seemed very confident that he would win the King's Cup again."

Yusef nods. "When the competition first began, it was equal between the two teams, but now the Royal Stables are not so big, while the Mounted Police have grown in size. They outnumber us ten to one, but that does not stop Bashir from boasting about his victories."

"What does Santi think?"

"Santi pretends not to care," Yusef says, "but he would love to beat Bashir so that the King could say with pride once more that his Royal Stables have the best horses and bravest riders in the Kingdom."

Yusef holds Bree while Haya mounts up and when he lets the reins go the bay can hardly contain her excitement. She skips and dances through the courtyard to the driveway where Zayn waits for them, mounted up on a big grey stallion called Claudius. The sound of the two horses trotting in unison up the driveway, metal horseshoes chiming on the tarmac, fills Haya with joy. She is back at her beloved Al Hummar, and even though she feels utterly exhausted, she is also elated to be riding her horse once again.

"How far is this new track you are taking me on?" she asks Zayn, trying to keep the anxiety out of her voice.

"About two hours," Zayn replies. "Maybe an hour and a half if we canter most of the way."

Haya is not sure her strength will hold for such a distance. But then she feels Bree beneath her, so light and responsive to every touch, and she is struck by absolute faith in her horse. If Haya is tired then Bree will care for her and carry her home. As long as she is on the bay mare's back, she has nothing to fear.

They ride out towards the forest along rutted tracks between olive trees and Zayn asks Haya about boarding school. She tells him about the fat ponies at Badminton, and her good luck in meeting the Ramsays and learning how to showjump. She'd been jumping Grand Prix courses on Victorious when she left – but she does not tell Zayn about all the ribbons and cups that had been stacking up in her dorm room. "We should build a showjumping course now that I'm back," she says. "I want to school Bree properly, like the Ramsays taught me."

"Perhaps you can give me jumping lessons?" Zayn says hopefully. "There are no good jumpers in our team for the King's Cup – and it could be the advantage we need."

"Do we stand a chance?" Haya asks.

"It is not hopeless," Zayn says. "There are five contests in the event – the military parade, the tent-pegging, falconry, showjumping and vaulting. Bashir's team is certain to win the parade – they drill their horses every day to march in perfect unison. But in the tent-pegging, our riders are just as quick as theirs."

"What about the other events?" Haya asks.

"I am quite good at vaulting," Zayn says. "With practice, we might win that one, but I think Bashir will win the showjumping and the falconry. So it does not look good."

The forest track broadens out on the way home and there is a long stretch of gently undulating path beneath the trees where pine needles smother the ground. Here they canter the horses and Haya feels Bree's powerful strides beneath her. Bree is so easy to ride, it is like floating on air. All the same, Haya is terribly tired. Her legs feel like jelly and when Bree pulls with excitement she can barely keep a grip on the reins.

"Can we walk for a while?" she asks Zayn.

"Sure," he says. "Are you OK?"

"I'm fine," Haya insists.

As the horses settle down, she is thinking about Bashir and the cup and the team from Al Hummar.

"What if I were to ride?" Haya suddenly says. "The team is weak at showjumping and that is my strength."

"You want to ride?" Zayn is shocked at first, but then he sees the serious look on Haya's face.

"If you ride in the cup, you cannot just compete in one contest," he points out. "You will need to ride all of it."

"I'm a good gymnast, one of the best at my school," Haya says. "So I can learn to vault. And I've watched the tent-pegging. I'm sure I can learn that too."

Zayn smiles in amazement at her determination. "Then you should talk to Santi. Tell him you want to ride."

He picks up his reins. "The path gets wider round this next corner. Ready to canter?"

By the time they reach the stables Haya is feeling giddy and can barely stay upright in the saddle. As she dismounts, her knees give way and Zayn rushes to her side. He takes one look at the pallor of her skin, the faint perspiration on her brow and calls for Yusef.

"Please sit here," Yusef says, helping her over to rest on a hay bale against the wall of the yard. "Do not move, Your Royal Highness. Radi will untack Bree for you and settle her back into her stall."

"I can do it myself," Haya tries to insist. But she doesn't have the strength to stand, and when Santi organises a car to come and take her home, she doesn't argue.

Back at Al Nadwa palace Frances takes one look at Haya's pale skin and the dark circles underneath her eyes and orders her straight back to bed.

"I will have your dinner sent upstairs, Princess Haya," Frances says. She cannot resist adding, "I knew it was too soon for you to be racing about on horses."

"I'm not ill," Haya complains.

"Then why did your father fly all the way to England to bring you home?"

*

That evening Ismail the head chef sends her dinner up in the dumb waiter. Haya takes the silver lid off the dinner tray and sees her favourite foods all laid out for her – tabbouleh, hummus, upside down, and *mansef* and apple pie with cinnamon for dessert. She is just finishing the last of the pie when her father enters her bedroom.

"It is good to see you have your appetite back," the King says as he sits down on the side of the bed. "Frances said that you overdid it today. You should not have gone to the stables, you should be home resting."

"I had to see Bree," Haya says.

"All the same," her father says, "you need to get your strength back, Haya."

"Bree is my strength," Haya replies. "When I was homesick, I would shut my eyes and pretend that I wasn't in England, I was back in Arabia, and it was just her and me, galloping forever across the desert."

Her father has said nothing more about what happened at boarding school. And he hasn't spoken about sending her back there again when the new school year begins. Haya knows that one day she will have to leave once more, but right now she is back home, with Baba and Ali and Bree.

"Bree!" Haya suddenly sits up in bed, looking worried. "I need to call the stables. I didn't even feed her..."

"Calm down," her father says. "Santi called and said to let you know that Bree ate all her supper tonight."

"They mustn't give her too much," Haya says

anxiously. "If she overeats, she might get colic…"

"I think Santi knows how to feed a horse by now, don't you?" Her father smiles. Haya looks down at her blankets, too shy to meet his eyes.

"What is it?" the King asks his daughter.

"I was thinking about my sixth birthday, when you gave Bree to me. Do you remember?"

"I do."

"She was so tiny," Haya says. "An orphan with no one to care for her, so alone. When you said that she was mine, I felt so scared."

"You met the challenge," her father says. "The filly survived – thanks to you."

"I thought so at the time," Haya says. "But that's not the truth, is it?"

Her eyes gaze up, filled with tears. "You gave me this foal who completely relied on me and, for the first time, I did not think about Mama, or how much I hurt inside – I thought only of Bree."

"Sometimes caring for another living being can be the best way to get over our own pain." Her father takes her hand. "You were so lost, Haya. There was so much grief in you that no one could get through. But from the moment you saw that filly, your heart began to open up again, and you came back to me."

Haya's voice shakes as she speaks. "I always thought that I had been the strong one, caring for her. But I realise now that it was the other way round." The tears spill down her cheeks and Haya wipes them away with the back of her hand.

"I didn't save Bree," she says. "She saved me."

Chapter 16

Learning to Fly

Ever since returning to Jordan everyone at the palace has treated Haya as if she were some delicate flower. They want to wrap her in cotton wool and keep her in her bedroom. The only place where she feels normal is the stables. Here, they do not fuss over her. Santi understands and he knows that she is a real rider, not some fragile little girl.

Or at least she thought so, until now.

"Listen to me, Titch," Santi says. "The King's Cup is not a competition for twelve-year-olds! It is for grown men."

"I can ride as well as any man." Haya stands her ground.

"Maybe," Santi says. "But you are a girl. In the history of the King's Cup no girl has ever competed."

"Just because no girl has ever done it before doesn't mean that I can't," Haya replies.

"Titch, if it were up to me, I would let you ride, but there are rules…"

"Not for this," Haya says. "There are traditions, but that is different. Sometimes traditions are good and they must be kept, but sometimes things grow and change. Why should a girl not ride alongside men if she is good enough?"

Santi is flustered by her logic. "This is a very serious contest, Your Royal Highness. And a dangerous one…"

"I have dreamed of riding in the King's Cup all my life," Haya says. "Fate has brought me home and I know in my heart the time has come."

"It was not fate that brought you home, it was exhaustion," Santi says firmly. "Already I've had to endure a lecture from Frances after your dizzy spell. You are supposed to be recuperating, not riding. If you were to get injured – it would be unthinkable."

"But surely that is my decision?" Haya says.

"No," Santi replies gently. "It is my decision, Haya, and it is made. You will not ride in the King's Cup."

*

The best place to be when you are sad or angry is on the back of a horse. Haya knows she can count on Bree to make her feel better. She thought she could count on Zayn too, but now she is not so sure.

"I am not surprised Santi said no," he tells her as they hack out together through the hills.

"You agree with him?" Haya says.

"I didn't say that," Zayn counters. "But it is an extraordinary thing to ask. Santi has known you since you were just a baby. He cannot see that you are growing up, that you are ready for this."

"You think I am ready?" Haya asks.

"Not yet, Your Highness," Zayn says, "but you will be. Once we have done some training."

"What's the point in that? Didn't you hear me say that Santi will not let me ride?"

"So you're giving up?" Zayn says. "Wow, boarding school really changed you. The old Haya would never give up so easily."

Haya pulls a face. "Very funny."

But Zayn isn't smiling. "You teach me to jump," he says, "and I'll teach you to vault. Do we have a deal?"

Haya looks at him. Then she gathers up Bree's reins.

"Come on, there's a fallen log up ahead. I'll give you your first jumping lesson."

They spend the afternoon hunting out natural obstacles in the forest and Haya puts her experience at the Ramsays' yard into practice as she explains to Zayn about getting the horse in close to the fence and judging strides and distance.

Bree, meanwhile, is learning too. She has a natural jump, but no schooling. Small logs are perfect for her right now.

"It's not the size of the fence that matters," Haya tells Zayn. "The horse must learn first to be balanced and come in steadily."

Once they have mastered the simple obstacles in the forest, Haya takes the training into the arena and they begin to use the coloured poles, setting up a variety of fences: doubles then triples. They drill the horses through grids to make them think fast and move with athleticism. Zayn barely notices that the fences are going up until one day Haya points to a spread that he has just flown over on Claudius and says, "Do you see that fence you just jumped? That was a metre twenty."

On the days when they are not jumping, they practise vaulting. They begin with a basic manoeuvre.

"Rhythm is what matters, Your Royal Highness," Zayn tells Haya. "Always count the strides in your head."

One-two-three. As Zayn canters past her, Haya bounds forward like a gymnast about to tumble on the mat. She throws up her hands and he grasps them and lifts her high up beside him. In one deft move, Haya swings her legs so that she is astride Claudius and they are doubling. It was a perfect vault!

"You learn fast." Zayn is surprised. But Haya has trained on the mat, the wooden horse, the rings and the parallel bars for many years now so these moves are second nature to her. However, the first time she tries to do a backflip off Bree, the mare spooks out from underneath her as she vaults. Haya mistimes her dismount and lands hard on the ground.

"What is wrong with your arm?" Frances asks Haya at breakfast the next morning. She has noticed the Princess wincing as she lifts a heavy glass jug to pour some juice.

"Nothing, I am fine," Haya insists. If Haya had rolled up her shirtsleeves then Frances would have seen the purplish-green bruise that extends all the way from her wrist to her elbow.

To dampen Frances's suspicions, Haya stays at home instead of going to the stables. Her arm hurts too much to train properly anyway and she has homework that the school has sent her. More excitingly she also got a card from her schoolfriends yesterday. It has a picture of a cat with a bandaged paw and inside it says Get Well Soon. Claire has drawn a love heart containing the words *we miss you* and all the girls have signed it. There is a letter from Jemima too, telling her the news from Shepperlands Copse, and asking whether she would be coming back before the end of term.

Haya writes back to Jemima: *I am in training for a competition here in Jordan. It is called the King's Cup...*

*

For the past month, as Haya and Zayn have trained, Santi has kept half a wary eye on them, and one day he comes down to the arena with Ursula. Haya has been focused on gymnastic schooling for Bree. The mare has proven a quick learner and Haya has slowly taken the poles up a few centimetres each time. Now at last she is ready to tackle a proper course.

Haya has seven jumps set up in the arena – all of them at a metre twenty. As she canters into the first fence, she checks Bree back beneath her and then pushes the mare on with a cluck and a tap of her heels. Bree responds with ears pricked forward and they fly the first fence. At each jump after that the mare comes in on a lovely forward stride and they complete the course without so much as rocking a pole. There is clapping from the sidelines as Haya joins Ursula and Santi, letting Bree stretch out on a long rein.

"Very good!" Santi is impressed. "The mare jumps even better than her mother. You ride her well."

"Well enough to compete in the King's Cup?" Haya asks.

Santi frowns. "I thought you were over that idea."

"What idea?" Ursula asks.

"Titch wants to ride in the King's Cup," Santi says. "But I have explained to her that she is too young."

Ursula looks at him. "Santi! You know there isn't a man in your stables who could jump the course that Haya has just ridden."

"They can jump well enough," Santi grumbles.

Ursula shakes her head. "You are being stubborn."

"And what if I let the Princess ride and she gets hurt? What then?"

Ursula sighs. "She is not a six-year-old girl any more, Santi. You cannot protect her from living her life. If she wants to ride then let her ride."

Haya senses that now is her chance. "Please, Santi,"

she says. "I won't let you down. I was jumping even higher when I was in England – I did Grand Prix."

"This is no pretty showjumping contest like the ones that you rode back in England," Santi says. "There are other events too. Tent-pegging and vaulting, and what about the falconry? We still have no one in the team who can compete in this event."

"Zayn and I have been training for the vaulting," Haya says confidently. "And I will compete in the falconry too."

Santi looks surprised. "You have a falcon?"

"Well, actually, not yet," Haya says, "but I am getting one, very soon." Her heart is pounding in her chest.

"Oh, come on, Santi," Ursula says. "You know she would be a great addition to the team."

Santi sighs. "Even if I say yes, it is impossible. Bashir will object."

"I'm not so sure that he will," Haya says. "How would it look if Bashir tried to stop me competing? Like he is so scared of being beaten by a girl that he would complain about me in public to the judges!"

Santi laughs. "You are right," he says. "And I would love to see the look on his face when you take to the field against him and his men."

"Please, Santi," Haya says. "All I want is to help you bring home the King's Cup for Al Hummar."

"You understand what you are taking on?" Santi looks serious. "This is a brutal tournament, with no holds barred. It is a battle and Bashir has an army."

"Well," Haya replies, "now you have me and Bree."

Chapter 17

The Sakret

At breakfast in the Blue Room the next morning the King is reading the morning paper when Haya pushes aside her plate and summons up the courage to ask him.

"Please, Baba, can I have a falcon?"

"To eat?" Ali asks with amusement.

Haya glares at her brother. "To train," she clarifies.

The King puts down his newspaper. "What has brought on this sudden urge? The last time we went hunting, I recall you were on the side of the hare."

"I have changed my mind," Haya says. "Please can I have one? I will feed him and look after him and train him myself."

"Falcons are not easy to handle," her father says. "They require skill and commitment."

"I looked after Bree well," Haya says. "Please, Baba?"

"I will speak with the head falcon trainer at the Royal Mews," the King says. "We shall see what he can do."

Two days later, a tall man dressed in a white thobe arrives at Al Nadwa, carrying a cage draped with a white sheet.

"Is it him?" Haya asks, trying to sneak a peek under the sheet.

Her father nods. "Would you like to meet him?"

Haya and Ali follow their father into the office and the falcon trainer puts the cage down on the pedestal by the window. He grasps the corner of the sheet and pulls it so that it falls to the floor and the bird in the cage is revealed.

He is small. Much smaller than Haya thought he would be, about half the size of her father's falcon Akhbar, a little less than thirty centimetres high, with drab, mottled feathers. Some of the feathers have fallen out in patches, as if he has been in a skirmish with a cat.

"He's got bits missing," Ali points out.

"He is moulting," the falcon trainer says. "He is

passagar, a young bird, and he has yet to grow into his adult plumage."

Compared to Akhbar this bird looks sickly. "Can he actually catch things?" Haya says, a little concerned.

"He is a sakret," the trainer replies. "A very popular bird, a good hunter, especially for desert hares. This is a good bird for you to begin with."

Haya is very grateful to have any falcon at all. The sakret may not be what she imagined, but she is not about to reject the bird that she is being offered.

"I'm going to call him Sama," she says. The name means Sky in Arabic, and Sama seems to love gazing up with his amber eyes. He looks as if he is deep in thought, with romantic visions playing in his head.

The falcon trainer steps over to the cage, opens the door and slips a leather hood over Sama's head. The bird's little beak pokes out beneath it. He ties off the leather cords to keep the hood on tight and then attaches the leather jesses to both of the bird's legs.

"You must always leave the hood on when you are handling him at first," the trainer advises Haya. He nudges his leather-gloved fist up against the belly of the sakret and the bird hops on to it obediently. He withdraws his hand from the cage very slowly with the sakret still seated on his fist, the bird's claws clenched tight, digging into the leather of the glove.

The falcon trainer passes a smaller glove to Haya. "Here," he says. "Put this on."

When Haya nudges the bird in his belly, Sama steps obediently off his trainer's fist and on to Haya's.

The sakret feels so strange perched there on her hand. She tries to keep her elbow crooked and her forearm at a right angle to hold him steady, but the bird begins to fidget and turn around.

"He is quite heavy!" Haya says nervously. She is not sure how long she can keep holding him.

"You will get used to it," the falcon trainer insists. "Keep him with you as much as possible in the first few days so that he knows you are his master now."

Haya tries to hold her arm steady, but Sama keeps rocking about. He is cocking his head from side to side, as if he is searching for something he cannot see.

"Your Majesty," the falcon trainer says, "I have brought another bird with me today that you may wish to use for your next hunt. It is in the cage outside. Would you like to come and see it?"

The King looks at Haya. "Will you be all right here until we return? We will only be a moment."

"Yes, Baba," Haya says confidently.

In the office, Haya holds her arm stiff and waits. Ali peers at the sakret. Then he waves his hand in front of the tiny hooded head.

"He can't see you," Haya says.

"It must be awful being blind," Ali says. "Do you think maybe we should take his hood off?"

"OK, you do it," Haya says. She holds her hand as steady as she can while Ali loosens the leather straps on the hood and gingerly slips it off the sakret's delicate head.

The moment the hood is gone the sakret lets out an ear-splitting scream, and immediately launches himself from Haya's fist. Unfortunately for Sama, there is a window between him and the sky, and he thwacks into it with a hard bang and falls to the floor.

The falcon trainer is shocked to return a moment later and find the bird lying on the floor.

"Is he dead?" Haya is too scared to touch him.

"He is just stunned." The falcon trainer picks the bird up. "It's lucky that Sama is so small – if that had been Akhbar then he would have broken the glass and kept on flying!"

Sama is put back in his cage to recover.

"How long will it be before I can fly him to catch a lure?" Haya asks the falcon trainer as he is leaving.

"These things take time," he says. "You will know when he is ready."

This was true when Haya broke in Bree. But Haya doesn't have months to wait. She peeks under the sheet at Sama in his cage. "You need to be ready soon," she tells him. Time is the one thing they don't have.

*

That evening Haya tries to have dinner with Sama on her fist.

"You can't take a bird with you into the dining room!" Frances says.

"I have to take him everywhere with me," Haya insists.

"It's unhygienic!" Frances says. Then she spies Haya's arm, criss-crossed with talon marks.

"Haya! What have you done to yourself?"

"I'm fine," Haya says. "They're just scratches."

"Good gracious, child, they're open wounds," Frances says. "Did the bird do this?"

"It wasn't his fault," Haya says. "I had my glove on, but it doesn't go all the way up my arm. When I took his hood off, he tried to get away, but he still had the straps holding him on to me and he kind of panicked."

Frances shakes her head in disbelief. "I thought boarding school would civilise you," she sighs. "But here you are, covered in wounds and coming to dinner with a bird perched on your hand like some desert Bedouin!"

She means it as an insult, but Haya instantly forgets the pain of the scratches on her arm and swells with pride. Enduring a few scratches is a small price to pay to prepare herself for the King's Cup.

*

Now that Santi has agreed to let Haya ride in the King's Cup she will practise each morning with the rest of the team. But when Haya arrives at the stables for her first practice, something is wrong.

"What is going on?" Haya asks as Zayn leads out a grey Arab mare from the loose boxes and holds out the reins to Haya. "Where is my horse?"

"Santi asked me to saddle Hira for you," Zayn replies. "He wants you to ride her instead of Bree."

Zayn sees the look on Haya's face. "I'm guessing that he hasn't told you this?"

Haya shakes her head. "Wait here," she tells Zayn.

She finds Santi in the tack room, sorting through a tangle of bridles.

"Ah, Titch!" he says. "Has Zayn tacked up Hira for

you? I will be out there in a moment to organise the tent-pegging…"

"I'm not riding Hira," Haya says. "I'm riding Bree."

Santi stops what he is doing and turns to her. "Haya, Bree is still in training. Hira is an excellent tent-pegging horse. Very swift and experienced, the fastest that we have."

"Then Zayn can ride her," Haya says. "I will not ride any other horse but my own."

There is concern on Santi's face. "Titch," he says, choosing his words carefully, "we do not have much time, only a few weeks left to train. When we ride into the stadium, those grandstands will be filled with thousands of spectators. This contest is very important to them. Do you want them to think that you were only chosen to ride because you are the daughter of the King?"

Haya shakes her head. "Santi, I know how much this means to my people. When I ride into that arena, I carry their hopes with me. I wish only to bring honour and glory to my father and to the stables of Al Hummar."

"Then ride Hira!" Santi says. "She is a proven mare; she has competed in this contest many times. On her you will acquit yourself admirably. On a young horse like Bree there is too much of a risk. Maybe she will

go well for you, but we cannot know. She is untried in competition."

"I know that you are only trying to protect me," Haya tells Santi, "but I promise you that when the people see me in that arena they will know I am riding my heart out. And they will see me riding the horse that I raised and broke in myself. Bree is my horse and she is the only one that I will ride."

*

The grooms have cigarettes clenched between their teeth as they tack up their horses. The morning air is filled with smoke and the sound of their talk, but when Haya leads Bree through to join them, the men fall silent.

It is Yusef who speaks first. "Santi has told us you will be riding with us at the King's Cup," he says. And then his face breaks into a broad grin. "Welcome aboard, Your Royal Highness."

"You had better be as good at the showjumping as Zayn says you are," Attah adds, "because Radi is useless!"

"Hey!" Radi turns to him. "You are worse than me!"

He smiles at Haya. "It is good to have you on our team."

The grooms mount up and begin to head down the driveway. They ride with their reins hanging long and loose, sitting relaxed astride their mounts, laughing and teasing each other.

Haya and Zayn are the last ones to ride down to the arena. Bree jogs along, skipping from side to side, her horseshoes chiming on the tarmac, and Haya has to tighten the slack on her reins to stop her from tearing off.

"Steady, girl," Haya reassures the mare, but although her voice is calm, her stomach is in a knot. She is just as excited as Bree.

"What did you do to your arm?" Zayn asks. Her left arm above where the leather glove ends has become like a road map of scars from Sama's vicious attacks. This morning Haya took the sakret's hood off to feed him his breakfast and he went berserk, screaming and clawing.

"It's nothing," Haya says. "I'm fine."

Santi has two tea chests filled with long slender wooden javelins, their blunt ends sticking out, the sharpened points facing down. In the centre of the arena, he places a row of small squares of paper, no bigger than table napkins, on the ground, weighted down by pebbles so that the wind cannot blow them away.

The grooms separate themselves out into two groups at the far end of the arena.

"Princess Haya!" Yusef, astride his big grey, calls out

to her. "Come and join our team."

Haya rides Bree at a loping canter down to the far end of the arena. Radi is on their team too. Attah and Zayn are the opposition and Santi rides with them to make up even numbers.

Each man rides his horse up to the tea chest, grasping and pulling out a spear with their right hand, reins held in the left. Haya rides Bree forward. The mare snorts at the sight of the tea chest and backs off.

"Come on, Bree." Haya kicks her on, but Bree dances on the spot and refuses to go any closer.

"Here," Yusef says, "take mine."

He passes his spear to Haya and takes another from the tea chest for himself. The problem is solved, but Haya cannot help but think about Santi's offer of Hira. Bree looks at a tea chest full of sticks as if it is a mountain lion about to eat her. How will Bree cope on the day of the contest if Haya cannot even get her to do this simple task at a practice?

Haya has seen tent-pegging performed many times, but this is the first time she has ridden it herself. It is an ancient cavalry sport and the aim is to be the first to race and spear a piece of paper on the ground and carry it back to the start line.

The horses are ready. Bree is trembling, every muscle and fibre ready to run. "On your marks..." Santi begins, but before he can say anything more, Bree rears up on her hind legs. Haya reacts fast and flings herself forward on to her neck to keep from falling. She pulls the mare down and stays in the saddle, but her face is pale with fright.

"Are you all right?" Santi asks.

Haya nods. She takes up the reins tight. "On your marks..." Bree tries to rear again, but Haya is too quick for her this time. She spins the mare in a tight circle, regaining control.

"Go!"

Bree breaks into a gallop and alongside her so does Hira. Both mares are quick and they are matching each other stride for stride. Bree's breath is coming in huffy snorts, ears flat back against her head, but Hira is one stride quicker and it is Zayn who reaches his target first. He makes a stab at the paper and misses! Now it is Haya's turn and she plunges her spear deep into the ground.

She misses too.

Haya has to make another three stabs before she manages to get the paper speared and by the time she and Zayn cross the finish line Santi has put away the

stopwatch, shaking his head.

Yusef rides over to her. "You hold the spear as if it were a stick," he says.

"It is a stick," Haya says.

"No," Yusef says, "you must think of it as if it were your own arm. You should hold it like this, do you see? Now hang low off the saddle and reach out to the paper as if you were about to grasp it in your hand."

As she gallops the next time, Haya imagines her arm reaching down to the ground, the target touching the tips of her fingers, and this time when she pulls her spear back up she is delighted to see the white piece of paper fluttering at the end.

"I did it!"

From that moment onwards the spear is a part of her and she never misses.

*

Haya is in the kitchen on her hands and knees behind the stove when Ismail comes in.

"Have you lost something?" he asks.

"No," Haya says. "I am checking the mousetraps."

She has already checked the one in the pantry and it was empty. The one behind the stove, however, does not disappoint her. These are live traps and inside, looking out with bright eyes, is a small grey field mouse. Haya reaches down and picks the trap up with the tiny creature still inside. She examines the mouse, looking at its tiny whiskers, the small, dark glassy eyes, and feels a pang of guilt for what she is about to do. Then she upends the trap into the leather pouch that she is carrying, so that the mouse drops into it, and puts the trap back into position and heads upstairs.

She is careful to shut the door quickly after her as she enters the bedroom. The curtains are drawn and in the half-light she can just make out the sakret sitting on his perch.

"*Sahhh-ma!*" He is wearing his hood, but he cocks his head at the sound of her voice. Haya does not go to him straight away. First she prepares herself, slipping on her leather glove and taking the squirming mouse out of the leather pouch. She wishes, not for the first time, that sakrets were vegetarians. She holds the mouse in her gloved left hand and goes over to the bird.

"Sama," she says, slipping the hood off his head. "Come and have dinner."

She holds her hand further away from the perch than she did last time she fed him. Small steps, a little further each time. That is what the falcon trainer told her.

He came to the palace two weeks ago to check on Haya's progress with Sama. She had been hoping that the falcon trainer would be pleased with her efforts, but he took one look at Haya, saw the fresh scratches on her left arm, and the sakret bare-headed and screaming on his perch and shook his head in dismay.

"You will ruin this bird," he told her firmly. "Why is he not wearing his hood?"

"I... am trying to make Sama happy," Haya said. "It seems wrong to leave him with a hood on. I want him to look me in the eye so we may be friends."

"I understand," the trainer said. "But this will not produce the results you crave. Sakrets are wild creatures. Only if you take away their eyes and make them blind can they submit and become as one with you. Your bird must wear his hood at all times, especially when he is on your fist. Do you carry him?"

"Not much," Haya admitted. "Frances won't let me. She says he's dangerous and he makes too much noise."

The falcon trainer frowned. "Would you leave a puppy alone in a room to howl? So it is with this sakret. Sama must be your constant companion." He looked at the bird, still screaming on his perch. "I will write you a list of what to do," he said, "but you must follow my directions. With luck, it is not too late and the bird may still be trained."

Since the visit Haya has tried to follow his advice. She has carried Sama everywhere, and has been feeding the bird by hand, calming his screaming. Until two days ago Sama fed with his hood on, but slowly Haya has been removing it again and now, little by little, she is teaching the bird to hop forward off his perch and come to her hand to eat.

"Here, Sama," she says softly, showing him the mouse in her gloved left hand. "Come on. It's your favourite."

Sama beats his wings and lifts off from the perch; he is in mid-flight when the door to the bedroom swings open.

"What on earth…? Why is it so dark in here?"

At the sight of Frances in the doorway, Sama lets out an ear-splitting scream.

"Shut the door!" Haya tells her. "You're scaring him."

"He's the one screaming at me!"

"Sama is having his dinner," Haya says.

Frances peers suspiciously at the object clutched in Haya's fist.

"Oh my lord!" Frances recoils. "What is that?"

"A mouse," Haya says. She sees the look of horror

on Frances's face and can't help goading the governess. "Here." She thrusts the mouse closer. "See?"

Frances jumps back with fright. Then she regains her composure. "Honestly." She shakes her head in disbelief. "Why can't you have a budgie like a normal girl?"

"If I had a budgie, Sama would eat him," Haya points out.

"This is ridiculous." Frances is flustered. "No more vermin in the palace. This bird of yours must be fed outside from now on, is that clear?"

"Yes, Frances," Haya replies.

She is not going to argue with the governess with the King's Cup so near. It is better to endure the telling-off than risk provoking Frances's wrath.

Sama, however, does not know how to hold his tongue. As Frances leaves, he lets out one last scream at the governess. Then, with two flaps of his wings, he lifts up and lands on his mistress's fist.

Chapter 18

The Shaved Bear

Haya has a photograph of her mother, taken back in her days as a champion waterskier. Her Mama was always the smallest and the lightest in her waterski team and that is why she was chosen to be the one to climb to the top of the human pyramid, riding high on the broad shoulders of the other skiers. Now it is Haya's turn to do the same, but not on water, *on horses*.

"Are you ready?" Yusef asks her. Haya is riding bareback, doubling behind Yusef on his big grey stallion, and now, as Radi pulls up close beside them on his horse, she knows it is time.

"Hup!" Radi says. And in one swift manoeuvre the grooms make their move. They stand up in unison, the two men balanced barefoot on the backs of the horses. Slowly Haya gets to her feet and as the horse keeps cantering beneath her she begins to climb. She uses Yusef's hip as the first rung in her human stepladder, placing her other foot across the narrow gap between the two cantering horses so that she is straddling thin air, one foot on Yusef, one foot on Radi.

Up she climbs, until she is on their shoulders, her arms up above her in the air like a circus performer! She holds the pose for a moment longer, waving to the imaginary crowd from the top of the world. There is a smattering of applause and she looks over to see Ali watching from the sidelines.

"What did you think?" Haya asks him.

"It is a very good trick," Ali says. "But didn't Bashir do it last year?"

Ali is right. Bashir's team have also mastered the pyramid.

"If we're going to beat them then we need something even better," Zayn says.

"Haya is a good gymnast," Ali says. "Why don't you do a handstand, Haya?"

"On a *horse*?" Zayn says.

"Sure," Ali says. "She can do one on a wooden horse

– why not a real one?"

Very soon the King's Cup will be upon them and the vaulting is now the most vital event. There are five flags in the contest and to win they must take three. One of those flags is the parade and there is little doubt that Bashir's team will beat them. Then there is the tent-pegging – and even Santi says that this contest will be neck and neck.

Haya is hopeful that she can take the flag in the showjumping. She only wishes she were as confident about the falconry. Sama is a very unreliable bird. She has worked hard for many hours trying to train the sakret, but with the contest just one week away, she still has him always on the long string and she daren't let him fly free. If she lets him loose, she worries he will disappear and never be seen again.

Sama's behaviour at the palace is dreadful. He is still prone to screaming when Haya feeds him, ear-splitting shrieks that bring Frances running every time. And Haya has fresh scratches up her arm yet again from yesterday when he chose to attack her instead of a tasty titbit she had brought him. She cannot rely on Sama, so that leaves only the vaulting – this they must win.

One-two-three. In the arena at Al Hummar, Haya rides

Bree forward, counting the canter strides out loud. She is bareback, dressed in cotton shorts and a T-shirt with bare feet and no helmet because it would get in the way when you are doing a handstand.

Bree's hoofbeats pound in time with Haya's heartbeat, steady and regular. "Good girl, Bree." Haya swings her legs and windmills her arms. She does this for a minute or two to get Bree accustomed to her movements. The mare must learn not to be distracted by the rider on her back. She must keep the canter, no matter what.

One-two-three, one-two-three. Haya's concentration is total. She lets go of the reins so that they hang around the mare's neck and now Bree has nothing holding her, she is free, yet still she keeps the canter rhythm. Haya spreads her arms out to the sides like an aeroplane. *One-two-three, one-two-three.*

"Good girl!" Haya says again. She's practised this part countless times and keeps Bree in the canter with no reins and her arms outstretched. But until now Haya has not been ready to try what comes next. Today is the day. She cannot put it off any longer.

One-two-three. Bree canters up the long side of the arena and Haya lowers her arms back down and places both hands in front of her on Bree's withers. Her fingers splay wide to help her to balance as she puts all her weight into her upper body. She is now poised like a gymnast about to perform a trick on a wooden vaulting horse. But Haya's horse is not made of wood, Bree is alive. *One-two-three. One-two-three.*

There is a metronome in her head keeping the beat. *Steady, not yet.* Haya hesitates for just a moment and then, as the mare's hind legs swing forward, she makes her move. Her arms stiffen and thrust as she pushes herself up in one swift movement, levering with her legs pushing away from Bree's sides, swinging her hips and tucking her knees underneath her so that now she is on her hands and feet, crouching on the mare's back as if she were a cat.

Keep the canter, one-two-three.

Haya looks down and sees the mare's shoulders plunging up and down beneath her, and the ground rushing by in a blur before her eyes. She jerks her head back up again. Much better not to look down! She keeps her head high staring straight ahead as Bree canters on with Haya perched precariously on all fours. She cannot stay like this for long without falling; she needs to execute the next move.

One-two-three. This time, on the third stride, Haya

pushes off. Her hands splay on the withers once more, gripping for dear life as her feet kick off, pushing her legs straight up into the air.

Immediately she knows it is not good. She was not strong enough in the kick to get enough height with her legs. And even if she had got her legs up, her hands are the real problem. Her palms are damp with perspiration and she panics as she feels them sliding down either side of the withers, her grip collapsing away beneath her. She loses her balance and comes crashing down, managing just in time to push herself hard away to the left-hand side so that she does not fall on top of Bree.

Everything goes into slow motion as the ground rushes up to meet her. She is falling head first and all she can do is stick out her arms to take the impact.

The ground is hard from the summer sun and she hits it with surprising force, taking the brunt of the blow on her hands. She lies there for a moment gasping, unable to believe her good luck. Her wrists ache from the ground-shock, but she gives them a shake and thankfully knows immediately that nothing is broken.

"Are you OK?" asks Zayn.

"I'm fine," she says, taking his hand and getting back up on her feet.

"It looked like you were going to do it this time," Zayn says encouragingly.

"It's my hands," Haya says. "Her coat is too slippery and my palms get sweaty and then I lose my grip."

"The riders that perform this in Spain have broad backed horses to balance on." Zayn is reading her mind. "Maybe an Arab is too skinny for a handstand?" Perhaps Haya is asking the impossible to try the same feat on a narrowly built mare like Bree?

"Do you want me to stay here while you try it again?" Zayn asks.

Haya grabs Bree by the bridle. "No," she says. "I'm taking her back to the stables."

There is no use trying again. She can't keep falling off head first like that. If she breaks a bone, she won't be able to compete. She will have to figure out a way to master the handstand in safety before she gets back on Bree.

For the rest of the afternoon, Haya practises in the courtyard. She can do a handstand on the compacted dirt surface of the yard and hold it perfectly with her legs straight in the air for at least ten seconds. She can even walk a few steps on her hands if she tries. But the ground is different to being on Bree. The mare's coat is so smooth, her shoulders so narrow. Haya needs to learn somehow to keep her grip on the mare's sleek withers or she will never master it.

*

Two days later, as Haya is walking up to the entrance of Al Nadwa palace, she looks at the stone lions standing sentry at the top of the stairs. Perhaps she should practise her vaulting on them? They are a low height, not quite so bad if she falls. Then again, they are right above the stone stairs, which would make quite a gruesome dent in her head if she fell. Also, the lions are too easy and not at all slippery. What she needs is something that is exactly like Bree, only on the ground.

She is walking down the hallway past the portraits of the Kings when she passes her father's office. The door is open a little and she wonders if he is in there working. "Baba?" She pokes her head in. Her father is not there, but lying in front of her is the solution she has been seeking.

The bearskin rug is spread out on the floor – paws pointing north, south, east and west, the great head of the creature looking straight at her father's desk. Haya shuts the door behind her, slips off her shoes and steps on to it. The thick brown fur feels deliciously bristly beneath her soles.

Haya walks to the middle of the bear and then raises both hands over her head and tilts up into a handstand. Her fingers plunge into the rug as she kicks her legs up.

She does a very good handstand. Too good. The bear fur is longer and shaggier than Bree's coat and Haya can grasp it with her fingers. Also, the floor beneath the rug is flat, not at all slippy like Bree's sloping withers.

Haya leaves the office and goes upstairs to find Ali in his bedroom.

"I need your help," Haya says to him.

Ali looks up from his comic book. "With what?"

"I need the bearskin out of Baba's office. It is too heavy for me to carry – will you help me?"

Ali narrows his eyes. "Are we going to get into trouble?"

"Probably," Haya shrugs.

Ali thinks for a moment. "OK."

At first, they try to carry the bear by rolling it up like a rug, but it is too bulky to get their arms round it.

"How about if we go underneath it?" Ali suggests.

"OK," Haya agrees. She takes the front half, putting her own head right beneath the bear's open jaws, wearing the rug as if it were a cloak with the large paws draped out over her arms. Ali takes the back end and they walk down the corridor like this, giggling. Haya thinks of the time they went to the theatre in London and saw a pantomime horse with one man playing the front half and another being the hind legs.

"I can't see," Ali complains after a while.

"Don't worry," Haya tells him. "Just follow me."

They take the bear down the stairs and out of the back door into the garden. They walk across the lawn and then down the stone stairs that lead behind the hedge to the greenhouse. They will be out of view of the palace here and this isolated spot has everything that Haya needs.

"Why are we taking the bear outside?" Ali wants to know.

"So I can practise my handstands on him," Haya says.

She looks round the greenhouse. The paddling pool is right where she last saw it, stored in the corner.

"Ali, can you pump up the pool? Not too much, just a little bit so it's kind of half full of air?"

Ali puffs and pants, working the pump to fill the inflatable pool while Haya checks out the lower garden. There is a low drystone wall that runs round its border. What she needs is a section of wall without any trees or plants in the way. She walks the perimeter and eventually decides on the perfect bit of wall, not too far from the greenhouse. She takes Ali's half-inflated pool and drapes it over the drystone rocks.

"What are you doing now?" Ali asks.

"I'm making a Bree," Haya replies.

They go back for the bearskin. This time they do not bother to wear it, they just drag it along the lawn and then fling it over the paddling pool.

"It looks good," Ali says. "Very horsey."

"No." Haya shakes her head. "The fur is still too shaggy."

She sets off back over the lawn towards the palace.

"Where are you going?" Ali asks.

"Wait for me here," Haya tells him. "I won't be long."

In the palace, she is heading towards Ismail's kitchen to look for scissors when she suddenly has a much better idea. She changes direction and goes up the stairs, turning to the right at the top of the landing and heading for her father's bedroom.

"Baba?" No answer. Her father isn't here. She walks through his bedroom. It is a beautiful room, very big with an elegant bed made up in crisp white Egyptian cotton sheets, the walls papered in pale gold flock paper, and the carpet, thick and opulent in a pattern of dusky blue. Haya enters the marble bathroom and looks around. Above the basin there is a cabinet and she opens this and finds what she is looking for. Her father's electric shaver.

*

"Sorry, Mr Bear," Haya says as she flicks the switch on the shaver, "but you need a haircut."

"You're going to shave the bear?" Ali is wide-eyed.

"Not the whole bear," Haya says. "I'll just shave the bits where my hands are going."

The bear's fur is thick and it takes more effort than she expected. The electric shaver keeps getting clogged up and Haya has to stop and pull bits of hair out of it. In the patches where it has been shaved the bear is now short-haired and sleek. Haya shuts her eyes and runs her hand over the shaved pelt. It feels almost exactly like Bree.

It takes forever to shave enough of the fur away for a decent smooth patch where both her hands can fit. By then the shaver has well and truly jammed up with bear fur – it gives a pitiful whine and the blades rotate once or twice and then crunch to a stop. Haya winces as she realises her father probably won't be able to use his shaver any more.

Haya climbs up on to the wall and stands on the bearskin, draped over the paddling pool. The weight of her body makes the bearskin slip a little underfoot.

"I'm going to need to tie it down," she tells Ali. "We need some rope."

Luckily there is rope in the greenhouse that is perfect. This is all going so much better than Haya could have hoped. She lashes the bear's head behind the ears and then ropes down the back paws so that the rug and the paddling pool are now both harnessed firmly to the wall. She climbs onboard once more, twisting her feet to see if it will give. The rug stays firm. At last, she can begin her handstand training.

*

"She mutilated it!" Frances is livid. "A priceless bearskin totally ruined by her childish games!"

Haya does not see what all the fuss is about. It is only an old rug after all. In fact, it is positively ancient: it belonged to Nana. Besides, once it is on the floor, you hardly notice there are flat patches.

"I wasn't playing games, I was training for horse riding!" Haya says.

"This is what comes," Frances counters, "from not giving children firm boundaries."

Behind the mahogany desk the King looks up at Haya and the governess standing before him. He puts his pen

down on the stack of papers in front of him. He has been working through the night and his face is drawn and tired. He has been so busy of late it took him three whole days to even mention that the bear was missing.

"I'm sorry, Baba," Haya says, "I was trying to learn to do a handstand bareback on Bree, but I kept falling. I thought if I practised on the bear first then I could master it."

Her father frowns. "But why did you shave it?"

"The hair was too long. I needed it to be more like a horse."

Her father raises an eyebrow. "That's clever," he admits. "Very clever."

Haya casts a sideways look at Frances as if to say 'Hah!' And then her father shakes his head. "You are grounded."

"What…?" Haya is confused. "But you said it was clever!"

"Haya, you knew it was wrong to do that to the rug, didn't you?"

"Yes, but…"

"Frances is right. You need to learn from this, Haya. You must think about what you did. You are grounded for the rest of the month until you leave again for the new term at boarding school."

Outside her father's office with the door shut behind them Frances turns promptly away from Haya and begins to walk towards the kitchen.

"I wasn't trying to ruin the rug, I was training..." Haya protests.

The governess stops. She turns back round.

"Do you really think this is what your father wants?" Frances's eyes are cold and cruel. "He is trying to run a Kingdom and here you are, a tomboy nuisance with mud on her knees and horse chaff under her fingernails, causing trouble again with your filthy horses. You should hear the talk around the palace, about the way you behave. Hanging around at the stables. It's disgraceful."

Haya is horrified. "But I am in training! The stablehands are my friends."

"It's entirely inappropriate – I cannot understand the purpose of all this training," Frances huffs.

"Oh, here it comes!" Haya is enraged. "Is this the bit where you tell me how I should behave like a proper lady?"

"I rather think we all gave up on that vain hope a long time ago," Frances says. And then she adds in a cold voice, "Your mother would be so disappointed." And with her insult thrust to the hilt, she turns her back on Haya and walks away.

Chapter 19

Daughter of the Wind

"Frances is a stupid meany." Ali is lying on Haya's bed, watching his sister stalk back and forth across the bedroom as if she were a panther prowling her enclosure. She has told her brother what Frances said to her yesterday in the corridor, what she said about Mama. It is typical Frances. She always knows how to inflict the most hurt. She never cuts a fresh wound; she just likes to pick at the same painful scab, over and over.

At the stables Zayn will be setting up the showjumping practice course and Haya should be helping him, but here she is wearing a groove in her bedroom carpet.

"Why don't you go out of the window like last time?" Ali suggests.

Haya shakes her head. "Frances is bound to expect it. I'd get caught and be double-grounded."

"Well, just tell Baba then," Ali says. "If he knows it was all for the King's Cup, he might let you ride."

"Or he might decide that he does not want the shame of having a tomboy for a daughter!" Even as she says it, Haya feels awful, snapping at her brother. None of this is Ali's fault. But she is still sore from the sting of Frances's words. Is that how Baba sees her? Is she really such an embarrassment?

She throws herself down on to the bed beside Ali.

"All this time when I was training," Haya says, "I was so excited. All I could think about was how I was going to surprise Baba. I would ride into the stadium on Bree and wave up at him in the Royal Box, and he would be so proud of me because I was his daughter, riding for the glory and honour of the Royal Stables. All I wanted was to make him proud. Now there is nothing to ride for."

"So you're not going to compete?" Ali asks. "But the King's Cup is tomorrow!"

"The team is better off without me," Haya says. "They were probably just trying to be nice letting me ride anyway. Daughter of the King – gotta do what she says. They don't need a girl getting in their way."

Ali stands up. Haya narrows her eyes. "Where are you going?"

"Nowhere," Ali says unconvincingly.

"Ali, don't you dare!"

"What?"

"You can't tell Baba, Ali. It will only upset him. I've done that enough already."

"You haven't! Don't listen to Frances. You should tell him!"

Haya looks at her brother. "Promise me you will not tell Baba."

Ali sighs. "I promise." He picks up his football lying beside the bed and heads for the door. "I'll see you later."

*

Haya spends the morning in her bedroom with her treasure box. She takes the objects out one by one, arranges them on her bed: the sunglasses, the tape cassettes, the seashell and the pebbles. She picks up the braid of Bree's black tail hair and feels the tears well. When Santi and Zayn load the horses on to the truck tomorrow for their journey to the stadium, Bree will be left alone in her loose box. Already the mare must be wondering why she hasn't been taken out for her morning workout; she will be whinnying her head off, calling to the other horses.

"Haya?" Ali pokes his head round her door. She quickly gathers up the contents of the treasure box and shoves the lid on, sliding it back under her bed.

"What?"

"Baba wants to see you downstairs in his office."

"Ali, what have you told him?"

"I haven't told him anything! I promised, didn't I?"

Haya's feet move slowly, one step at a time down the staircase. Has Frances been talking to Baba again? What has she said now?

The door to her father's office is shut and she can hear the muffled sound of voices on the other side. Her father is in a meeting. She stands there, uncertain, hand poised over the handle, when the door opens in front of her and she is looking up at the tanned, broad face of Santi.

"Hello, Princess Haya," Santi says. "Your ears must have been burning. Come in."

The door swings wide and Haya can see Zayn. Her first thought is that Frances has complained to the King about Haya spending too much time at the stables. Then the door swings open further and her assumption is confirmed. Haya can see the rest of the grooms standing alongside Zayn. All of them are bunched together, hands clasped in front of them, looking very stiff and uncomfortable about being in such a grand space in their dusty stable clothes. It is quite strange for Haya to see them here, as if her two lives are suddenly colliding in the one room.

"Haya," her father says, "Santi and his grooms have been speaking with me. It appears that you omitted to tell me that the reason you shaved my bearskin rug is because you were training to ride in the King's Cup?"

Haya looks at the brave faces of the men. Are they all in trouble because of her? "It wasn't their fault," Haya says. "I was the one who thought of the bearskin. Santi didn't even know about it."

"This is not about the bear." Her father looks grave. "Santi tells me that you did not turn up for training at the stables this morning. He would never have known the reason for your absence if Ali hadn't gone to see him."

Ali! So that was where he went!

"Really, it is not good enough, Haya," her father continues. "When you commit to a team, you must not let them down..."

She cannot believe what she is hearing. "But I am grounded!"

"You will be disciplined appropriately for what you did to the rug," her father says. "But these men should not pay for your mistake. You have a team who are relying on you and you must honour that obligation."

"So you are allowing me to ride?" Haya cannot believe it.

Her father gives a wry glance at his grooms. "I think I would have a mutiny on my hands if I did not say yes. You had better change now into your jodhpurs – I believe you have a jumping practice."

In her bedroom, Haya dresses in a daze. She has grabbed her boots and is about to head downstairs again when there is a knock at the door. It is her father.

"Santi and his men are outside in the truck. They will take you with them to Al Hummar," he says.

"I should go, Baba," Haya says, grabbing her sweatshirt. "I have kept them waiting enough already today."

"They can wait a moment longer I am sure," her father says. "I want to talk to you." He gestures for her to take a seat on the bed beside him.

"I thought you told me everything, Haya. Why did you not tell me about this?"

"It was going to be a surprise," Haya says. She realises how silly it sounds now.

"Santi tells me that you are the best rider in his team,"

her father tells her. "You know it took great courage for these men to come and see me today. They did it because they have great respect for you as a rider, Haya. They are depending on you. Santi thinks for the first time in a long time the Royal Stables can defeat the Mounted Police."

He expects her to look pleased, but instead, Haya looks like she is about to burst into tears.

"I'm sorry," she says.

"What for?"

"For everything. For being like this. I know the way that I behave, what I am, it isn't what you wanted," Haya says. "I disappoint you. I am not a proper lady, not like Mama. I wish I could be like her, but I'm not."

"Haya," her father says. "Do you know what made your mother a Queen? It was not her grace and good manners, it was her heart. She was so determined, so fearless. It is these qualities that I see when I look at you, Haya. You are her daughter in every way. She would have been so proud of you today, to see the way the men of our stables came to stand beside you. You inspire them, not because of your title, but because they can see who you are inside. This was your mother's great gift and you have it too, Haya."

Her father takes her hand. "You will be a lady one day

when the time is right. But when you go into the arena tomorrow, that is not the time. Bashir is ruthless and his team will not give any quarter in the arena. You will have to outride them to win."

"I am ready," Haya says. "I promise I will make you proud, Baba."

Her father smiles. "My daughter, you already have."

Chapter 20

The King's Cup

The stadium is built like the Colosseum. A circular sand arena bordered by a tall stone wall with tiered seating above so that the crowds can look down on the spectacle of this historic battle between the Royal Mounted Police and the Royal Stables of Al Hummar. Haya has been here every year with her father since she can remember. She has sat alongside him in the King's box, looking down at the golden sand below.

Today she sees the arena for the first time from the gladiators' point of view. In the darkened corridors of the stables beneath the grandstands she squints out into the bright sunlight. She can see the people filling up the stadium; there is a buzz of excitement as the crowd take their seats.

"Do you hear them?" she whispers to Bree. "They're going to be making a lot of noise today when we ride out there, but don't be afraid. They will be cheering for us, you'll see…"

Beneath her, Bree stamps her hooves against the concrete floor of the stable block, as if she is anxious too, as if she knows how much this means to Haya.

They are a team and yet Haya is only telling Bree half the truth. The crowds will celebrate if she wins today. But if she loses? This contest means so much to her people and she feels the weight of their hopes riding on her slight shoulders. Not only that, she knows that Frances and her followers will be out there today too, waiting like vultures to feast on her defeat. "There!" Frances will say triumphantly. "You see? A young lady of royal birth should not be riding. She should be at home, preparing for palace life, marriage and royal duty."

Well, Haya defies Frances and her narrow-minded conventions. When she enters the arena on Bree, wearing the colours of Al Hummar, she rides not only for the glory of Al Hummar, for the honour of her father, but for the right to choose her destiny.

A roar rises up from the crowd. Bree shudders and

Haya is shaken out of her thoughts. In the arena, the Mounted Police, led by Colonel Bashir, are about to parade before their King. Bashir is dressed in his full military kit, his khakis decorated with medals, and a red sash worn over his shoulder. In one hand he holds the reins and in the other the red and gold flag of the Mounted Police.

Bashir's horse is a chestnut, handsome and fine-boned with three long white stockings and a white blaze. The next two men also ride chestnuts and two more men bring up the rear on matching greys. The horses swing along at a marching walk. The noise of the crowds does not bother them. They are police horses, trained especially for such things. When they reach the Royal Box, they halt in perfect unison.

"Company, present arms!" Colonel Bashir shouts. His men all reach for their scabbards with their right hands, and in one swift movement their swords are unsheathed and raised in salute to their King.

In the Royal Box, the King salutes back. Haya can see Ali right beside him also dressed in official uniform, with Frances in the row behind, keeping a watchful eye.

The other occupants of the Royal Box sit directly in front of their King. There are four of them, old men with faces that are creased and furrowed by the sun, wearing white robes with their heads covered with keffiyeh. They are all great horsemen who have served their King and today these four sit in judgement to decide the outcome of the contest. There will be five events, and from these they will decree the winner.

"Company, salute!" The Mounted Police riders acknowledge their King once more and then Bashir pirouettes away, urging his horse into a canter. He leads his men as they turn in formation, tracking a half-circle around and fanning out once more, lining up side by side and pulling their mounts in unison to a halt. They march forward on the right rein, then the left, halt and pirouette. And, with a final wave to the crowds, they leave the stadium.

Now it is the turn of the riders of Al Hummar.

"Are you ready to go in?" It is Santi, standing beside her. He is dressed in chinos and a cotton chambray shirt. It is a hot day and it will get hotter.

Haya looks nervous as she gathers up her reins. She wears the blue and white colours of Al Hummar and her teammates line up behind her on their horses dressed in the same uniform. It was Yusef who insisted that Haya should be the one to lead them into the arena.

"You should do it, Yusef," Haya replied. "You're the head groom."

"And you are a Princess," Yusef replied, "which makes you the highest ranking among us. You must be the one to take us into the arena."

"I am twelve. I am too young."

"Your father was seventeen when he became King of a nation," Yusef replied, and with his words her courage leapt.

Haya gazes out across the golden sand. Once, a long time ago, she sat in the Royal Box beside her father and her Mama too. The Queen wore a green dress, a white straw hat and white-rimmed sunglasses. This is not Haya's own memory, although it feels as though it is. It is a photo she has seen. Her mother in the Royal Box at the King's side, so beautiful, smiling and waving. Her mother, forever young, untouched by time. Haya wishes so much that she were here today to watch her ride. She is determined to make her proud.

"We will both make our mothers proud today, Bree," she whispers to the bay mare moving restlessly beneath her. "You must do this for Amina."

Santi solemnly passes Haya the blue and white banner of Al Hummar. With each challenge won, a flag will be raised on one of the five poles. If they win, it is the blue and white of Al Hummar, but if they lose then Bashir's red and gold flag will fly instead.

"Are you ready?"

Haya nods.

"Then go, ride well and God protect you!" Santi says.

To the fanfare of trumpets, Haya urges Bree straight into a canter and the men of Al Hummar follow behind her across the sands. Swooping around the arena, she urges the mare to a gallop and the riders speed behind her, their horses' legs working like pistons in the sand. The blue and white flag flutters violently in Haya's hand, the wind whipping at it so hard that she has to close her fist tight to keep it in her grasp. They charge past the stands, racing as if their horses have fire in their tails.

The dramatic entrance receives a roar of approval from the crowd and Bree responds to their cheers, surging forward even faster. Haya looks back over her shoulder to see Zayn, then Yusef, Attah and Radi, all keeping up with her in perfect stride, riding single file at the gallop.

Up the centre of the arena the four riders fan out and draw alongside her to pull up dramatically and halt, kicking up the sand with their hooves as they skid to a standstill in a perfect row beneath the Royal Box. Haya looks up at her father and brother, the four judges stony-faced in the seats directly below them.

"Company, present arms!"

It is Haya's voice, high and sweet on the air as she gives the command. There is a titter from the crowd at the squeak of this young mouse leading her lions. Haya ignores the murmurs of amusement; she keeps her expression serene as she raises her flag and holds it out in salute. Her arm trembles from the effort of keeping it aloft. Beside her, the men draw their swords to salute their King. Their salutes are a bit raggle-taggle compared to Bashir's officers and Haya knows this will cost them. She can feel the beads of sweat forming on her forehead, the flag is so heavy. The King returns her salute and finally she can lower her arm. With relief, she hands the flag to the bannerman on the ground to carry to the Royal Box. Her muscles are spent. She has to try really hard to stop her arm from shaking as she takes up her reins.

"Company, to the left, march!" Haya's voice has more depth this time as she gives the order. The men fall into step behind her and she trots Bree, reins held in one hand, saluting the crowd with the other as she pushes the mare into a bouncy canter. Down the centre line at a canter they turn, then spin on their hocks 180 degrees so that they are facing the opposite way and Radi, who was at the rear, is now leading them. They split up, going this way and that, making two lines then crossing neatly between each other across the arena. As the riders pass back and forth in perfect time, Haya finds herself grateful for those boring quadrille classes with Mrs Goddard!

The energy of the crowd carries them as they gallop one more time around the perimeter, then fan out into a line and halt with precision in front of the King for their final salute.

Haya's father stands to acknowledge their efforts and she sees a faint smile play on his lips as his hand sweeps to salute his daughter. Beside him Ali screws up his face at her as he salutes. Haya manages to suppress her grin as she turns Bree and rides at a gallop once more to leave the arena. The riders storm back into the stables, their horses blowing hard from the gallop. Haya's face is flushed and sweat soaks her cotton shirt.

"Was it OK?" Haya asks Zayn. "Did you see my hand wobbling on the flag? I couldn't hold it straight…"

"You were great," Zayn reassures her.

"It was brave riding," Santi says as he joins them, "but

Bashir was very polished. We will wait and see what the judges think."

In the corridors of the stables the riders crowd together and stare out at the five flagpoles in the arena, waiting for the first flag of the tournament to be raised. Will it be the blue and the white of Al Hummar? The riders are silent; there is only the snorting and stamping of the horses as they watch the bannerman take his order from the judges and the flag is attached and hoisted high. A cheer goes up from the crowd.

It is red and gold.

"Remember Bashir's men drill like this every day," Santi reassures his team. "We never expected to take them in this challenge."

"If I hadn't let the flag wobble..." Haya says. But Santi shakes his head.

"There is nothing to be gained by looking back, picking the garment apart to look at the stitches. We must focus on the next challenge. There are still four flags to be won."

*

Three riders have been chosen from each of the teams to race in the tent-pegging and the ululations of the crowd call the six chosen riders out on to the golden sands.

Bree is quivering with excitement. She knows the race is coming. She is ready to explode.

"Not yet," Haya tells the mare trembling beneath her.

"Riders, on your marks…"

The moment she hears the word "Go!" Bree explodes forward. They are the first off the line as the thunder of hooves rocks the stadium. This is nothing like their training; riders are jostling and shoving as they gallop and nobody sticks to their line. To the right of her, a rider on a chestnut crowds Bree, and Haya swerves, only to encounter the rider on a grey mare to her left.

"Get out of my way!" Haya shouts. But the Mounted Police rider ignores her entreaty and rides her off her line.

Haya almost loses her balance and grabs at a hank of mane to stay onboard as Bree's stride falters. They have lost ground, but they recover as Bree stretches out, her strides devouring the ground. Haya stands up in her stirrups and rides like a jockey, perched off the mare's back to let her run. Bree has her ears flat back as she gallops for all she is worth.

The grey mare is right in front of them and running fast too. There is nothing in it, no more than a stride, as Haya eyes her target. She drops her right shoulder low to the ground, her arm poised with the spear as if she were about to plunge into the water after a fish. In one swift motion, she thrusts the spear down, piercing the paper clean through the middle. Then she raises the stick aloft, her fluttering prize on the end, turning Bree and spurring her towards home. Behind her two of the Mounted Police riders have missed their target and are left circling a second time, but the rider on the grey mare and Zayn and Yusef have all hit their targets. They race close behind her.

Haya leans down low over Bree's neck, urging her to the finish line. She can hear Bree's snorts coming in thick rasps. Haya knows that the grey mare is not far behind them. She risks a quick glance over her shoulder. They are even closer than she thought! But the finish line is close and the crowd are roaring. She will be first to the line!

As she crosses, just ahead of the grey mare, she stands in her stirrups and holds her spear aloft, but suddenly there is a groan of dismay from the grandstands. Haya does not understand, but then she looks up at the stick in her hand. There is no paper! It must have flown off before she reached the line. Beside her the rider on the grey mare raises his own spear high, the white paper still intact. He pumps the air with his fist to the cheers of his supporters.

Bad luck. That is what her teammates say to Haya back at the stables. But no one ever says it was good luck when you win, do they? If only she had speared the paper more cleanly, held the stick lower as she galloped, then maybe the paper wouldn't have flown off. Maybe…

"Never mind," Santi tells her firmly. "Focus on the next challenge if you want to win."

But the two red and gold flags of the Mounted Police fly in her face and sting like a slap across the cheek. The next challenge is crucial. There are only three flags left and they have no more chances.

Chapter 21

The Silver Accord

Two drops of blood fall from Haya's hand to the golden sand. Thick and dark like treacle. She holds the severed bird wing out at arm's length as she inspects it. It will make a good lure. She gives it another shake to get rid of any more stray droplets, then she binds the long string around to secure the wing, making sure to knot it tight. Then she puts out her arm to Sama on his perch and when the bird feels her nudge against his belly he hops obediently on to her gloved fist.

"Come on," she says, holding the sakret aloft. "It's our turn."

There are five flags and they have already lost two. And here she is, in the arena with Sama, hoping that the sakret will deliver their first victory. She feels the weight of the bird on her hand. Sama has grown much heavier in these past weeks. He has all his adult feathers and has nearly doubled in size. This week Haya has flown him off the long string three times and each time he has returned to her hand. But that was in the garden at the palace; they are not at home any more.

Haya shoves the bird-wing lure back into her shoulder bag. Then she steps out with Sama into the arena and walks to the centre of the ring where a wooden post has been erected in the sand. She lifts Sama to the post and he hops obediently off her fist on to the perch.

Sama is wearing his special hood today, the one that the falcon trainer gave her for the occasion. It has a crown of colourful feathers that stick up from the centre, as if the sakret were wearing a pineapple on top of his head. Haya thinks he looks very grand, but she suspects that Sama feels ridiculous. A plain leather hood would suit him better.

Haya strikes the leather braces and removes the hood with a deft pluck, pocketing it with her right hand. The bird's amber eyes go wide at the sight of the stadium, filled with a thousand faces staring down at him. "It's OK, Sama," Haya tells him. There is a hush in the air, the atmosphere heavy with expectation as Haya steps away from the sakret and begins to step out her strides until she is twenty metres away from the wooden post.

Sama cocks his head and watches as Haya pulls the lure out of her shoulder bag. She tosses the bird wing out to her right, keeping hold of the string in her gloved hand, guiding it with the other hand. She begins to swing it like a cowboy starting off a lasso. As the string goes taut, she sweeps the lure in a low circle beside her. In ever-increasing circles, Haya eases out the string until the bird-wing lure looks as if it is flying on its own. It rises up and arcs into the sky.

Looking up from his perch, Sama catches sight of the lure, gives two swift wing-beats and lifts up into the air. He is airborne so fast, Haya must be careful that he does not strike before she is ready. This is meant to be a dance between the handler and their falcon. Sama must only take the lure when she is ready to give it.

In the sky, Sama tracks a circle above the lure and then stoops, diving at it with talons outstretched. Haya anticipates him and alters her trajectory. Sama has to pull up in midair and turn to attack again.

Haya is a matador and Sama the bull as he makes

another play to snatch at the bird wing. Once again she anticipates and correctly adjusts the lure's flight path to keep it tantalisingly out of reach.

Their dance looks fluid and effortless as Haya makes Sama duck and dive, but she can feel the sweat forming beads on her brow. She has the lure at full length now and she knows that the longer she plays out the game, the more risk there is that she will make a mistake and the lure will crash down. Or worse, the bird will become bored or be startled by the crowd and vanish into the air never to return.

So, just after she jerks the string and makes Sama stoop to a particularly challenging line, she throws it up again, swinging the lure like a propeller blade. She relinquishes her hold and lets it fly free from her hand. The lure reaches the top of its trajectory and hangs above Sama in midair. With a swift dart, the sakret takes his quarry, grasping the bird wing in his claws.

Haya holds her breath as she watches him dive from the sky, the wing in his talons. This is their final test. She holds her gloved hand out for him and whistles. Sama looks up and, in an instant, he takes flight. He returns to her, prey still grasped tight in his claws.

The drops of blood that fall on the sand are red, but

the third flag that is raised is the colour of the sky. The blue and white flag of Al Hummar.

*

Haya remembers what Santi said when she first told him that she wanted to ride in the King's Cup. *This is not some pretty showjumping contest like they have back in England.* Perhaps, if she had really listened, she would not be so shocked by the sight of the jumps that are being erected in the arena today.

The first is a warm-up fence, a straight rail with a ground line, set at just under a metre high. The next jump is a spread, almost a metre twenty, with a width intended to get the horses stretching out and using their frames. But it is the third fence at the centre of the arena that sends murmurs through the crowds at the stadium.

It is a spread with the top rails set at a metre forty – almost as high as the Grand Prix fences that Haya rode back in England. But the top rails of the spread are very wide apart at a width of a metre twenty.

"That is a huge gap," Haya observes as the lower rails are put in place on the jump stands. "They need to put flowers or straw bales or something underneath the spread. Otherwise the horses will try to treat it as a bounce stride and land between the rails."

"I don't think they're using flowers," Zayn says. He gestures towards the arena gates. "Look."

A silver car is being driven across the sand by one of Bashir's riders. It is a silver Honda Accord and its tyres cut like snakes into the soft sand, leaving tracks behind them. The driver swings the car out wide around the first fence, taking a route along the edge of the arena. Then he drives at a right angle straight towards the third jump.

Haya watches in disbelief as the car stops dead in the middle of the jump, parked between the two rails of the spread.

"You can do this," Santi says. "You've jumped higher than a metre forty at Shepperlands Copse."

"Not on Bree," Haya says.

"She can make the height. She has been jumping almost that big in the training sessions."

"Not over a car!"

"Do not think about the car, only think of the rails."

"How can I not think about the car," Haya asks, "when it is right there in the middle of the fence?"

The rules of this challenge are simple. Only one jump matters – the car. The riders are each given three chances to clear it.

Haya has seen a contest like this once before. It was

the puissance, a high-jumping competition at a horse show in Sussex. The Ramsays had taken her to the show and she stood on the sidelines with Jemima and Lucinda and watched as the stewards erected a huge wall out of big wood bricks. The wall was so high the riders couldn't even see over it as they approached.

The riders urged their mounts to take deep, powerful strides, collecting up so that their hocks were right beneath them to push off and make the height of the wall. That was when Haya realised that the big jumps shouldn't be taken in a fury of speed and adrenaline, but with ice water in the veins.

Haya also knows that jumping a car has different demands to a brick wall. When she approaches, she will need enough power in Bree's hocks to push up to make the height, but *also* enough speed to carry them over the width. If she gets it wrong then things will be very bad indeed. It doesn't matter what Santi says. If you land on top of it or crash into it, the results could be extremely nasty.

The excited crowd can't wait for the event to begin. Haya stands in the darkened stable corridor holding Bree's reins, looking out anxiously into the arena. "Are you watching?" she whispers to the bay mare. Bree gives

her head a shake at that moment as if to say that she is most definitely not.

"OK," Haya says to her, playing affectionately with Bree's forelock. "Maybe it is better if you don't look. But I am going to watch, OK?"

She is glad that the Mounted Police have chosen to go first.

"Have they started yet?" Zayn is puffing and panting, having run all the way here from the other end of the stable block.

"Not yet," Haya says. "The first rider is just about to go…"

The first rider into the ring is the man on the grey mare who beat them in the tent-pegging. He rides out at a frantic gallop.

"He's going too fast," Haya tells Zayn. "It's too wild and furious. That is not how you should approach this jump."

She is proven right a moment later when the grey mare does a power slide, slamming on the brakes right in front of the car. She does it two more times and the rider is disqualified.

Rider after rider it is the same. The Mounted Police do not seem to know how to tackle the car. They rush it too quickly or approach too timidly. By the time Bashir's turn comes the crowd are disillusioned and they think that no one is ever going to make the jump.

Haya does not want to watch Colonel Bashir take his turn. She is in the practice arena, warming Bree up over the cross rails. She hears the roar of the crowd as Bashir makes his approach and the groan of dismay as he too fails in his bid. There is silence as Bashir leaves the arena, shaking his head in dismay. All it will take for Al Hummar to win this flag is for one rider to make the jump. And their first rider in the arena is Haya.

Santi and Ursula are at the entrance waiting for her. "Remember," Santi says as she does up the strap on her helmet, "ignore the car. Your eyes must not go there. Keep them up, Haya, always above the rails – to where you want to go. If you look at the car, you are looking down and Bree will stop."

It is one thing to assess the mistakes of other riders when you are on the sidelines. Now that she is in the arena, Haya feels as though her training is trickling out through her ears. Can she keep it together? She picks up the canter and begins to circle. Stay calm, stay relaxed.

But it's a car!

She can do this. She has jumped this high before at the Ramsays' yard.

Yes, but never on Bree.

They canter in boldly to the first fence and Haya is only a few strides out when she feels the mare back off. Haya has been so preoccupied with the car that she is not riding on strongly enough into the first fence. Bree is going to refuse it! Haya gives the mare a firm nudge with her heels, sending Bree on just in time.

They are over! It was a little ungainly, but they are clear. Haya pulls herself together, preparing for the second fence. The crowd are hushed as they approach the spread and focus on the jump. This time Bree comes in on a lovely forward stride and flies it with ease. Haya gathers up the reins. Ahead of them lies the third jump, the wide spread, and beneath the rails, glinting in the sunshine, is the silver car.

Ignore the car!

Lining Bree up, she comes in at the jump. She is riding well, she can see the stride, she is holding the mare on her line, but then Haya looks at the silver car and hears the cries of the crowd. With all of those eyes upon her, a switch flips in her head. Suddenly Haya's confidence is gone. Doubt grabs at her gut.

Bree feels her rider's sudden hesitation and responds, instinctively backing off the fence. Their anxiety snowballs as horse and rider feed off each other's nerves. When Haya puts her legs on and growls, "Get up!" all Bree hears is the uncertainty in her voice.

At the last minute, just when she is supposed to jump, the mare reels back, suddenly forcing all of her weight to her hindquarters, throwing herself into a skid. Bree's hocks dig deep into the sand beneath her, but it is not enough to slow her down. There is a collective gasp as the mare barrels into the car, crashing into its metal doors, and bringing the rails of the spread tumbling all around.

Haya is flung upward with a violent jerk that catapults her clean out of the saddle. She flies up in the air and falls hard against the bonnet of the car. At that same moment the rails fall, smashing down right on top of Haya. One of them smacks her arm against the car, while another strikes a glancing blow off her helmet. Haya falls with the rails, tumbling from the car bonnet on to the sand.

Against the blue sky three flags fly: two are red and gold, one blue and white. They are the last thing Haya sees as she closes her eyes.

9PM, 24 AUGUST 1986

Hello, Mama,

It's me again; Baba has sent me upstairs to rest. I keep telling him that I am fine and he fusses too much. I have a bit of a headache, that is all, and not from the fall, but spending the day under the hot sun.

I suppose at the time my fall must have looked quite dramatic. Me lying there, so still on the ground. I was unconscious when they reached me. Ali says it is the only time he has ever known me to be quiet!

I remember waking up and thinking, *Why am I down here? Where is my horse?* And I must have groaned out loud because I heard someone say, "She's awake!"

I was blinking my eyes because the sun was shining right into them and I couldn't see. I felt someone putting their arms round me and I must have been a little bit dizzy because I could have sworn it was you. You were holding me and protecting me. I said your name. And then there were people crowded above me, blocking out the sun, and I could see that it wasn't you at all, it was her.

Frances was on her knees in the sand, cradling me to her bosom. I don't think the St John ambulance would have recommended this to be honest; I am not sure that hugging someone that tight is the recovery position. She looked so worried. Not that fake look of concern that I have seen her put on for Baba's benefit, but really, truly worried about me.

"Haya! Stay still. Help is coming. It's all right, you're going to be all right." That is what she said over and over. She was crying. I could see the redness and watery tears in her eyes. I tried to push myself up and that was when I felt the pain. It was like a knife stabbing into my right arm.

I never told anyone, but after you died, I used to play this game in my head. Well, not a game exactly. It was… well, I guess you would call it a negotiation. I wanted you back so badly, I got this idea in my head that I would make a deal with fate. I started bargaining

with my fingers at first, counting them off one by one, but I knew that it was not enough. Fingers are not a true sacrifice. And so I shut my eyes and offered fate my arm. Without it, I would never ride again, but I would have you back and it would be worth it.

I don't remember why I thought I could make this deal, handing over pieces of me until I could cheat fate. But your death makes no sense, so why would you expect me to be sensible? I was hurting so much and all I knew was that I wanted you back.

Most kids don't think about dying. They think they will live forever. But I know death and I know now that you cannot bargain with it.

After you died, I was so worried about losing Baba too. I was desperately afraid that an assassin's bullet would claim him, that it would find the way to his heart this time instead of bouncing off the medal on his chest.

One day, when I was very sad, Baba asked me what was wrong and I told him I was scared for him. He held me close and told me that he understood, that he would never want to lose me either, but I must not let death cast its dark shadow over me.

Baba said that when the bullet bounced off his chest

that day he lost his fear of death forever. He was alive against the odds and only fate could say when his day would come. Until then, he would live bravely in the service of his Kingdom and he would not dwell on it. Fate chooses its course for all of us and that cannot be altered no matter how much we wish we could change things. And if we believe that our fate is already settled, then there is no room for fear.

Fear was what I saw when Frances held me in her arms and I realised that is how Frances lives her life. She is afraid of everything – of picking up the wrong fork or hurting herself on a horse, of getting mud on the carpet or making the wrong friends. And that is no way to live.

You taught me to be brave, Mama. You did not let fear hold you back when you got on the helicopter to Tafilah. So, if I am brave today, it is because of you, and Baba.

My arm was still really aching, but when I tried to wiggle my fingers, I could still move them and I knew that nothing was broken. Taking a deep breath, I pushed myself up, freeing myself from her arms.

"Haya..." Frances looked so lost, it made me feel as if she were the one who needed to be helped, not me.

"I'm OK," I said. "I'm not hurt."

Later on, I wished I had said something nicer to her, just this once. But that is not how it is between Frances and me. Maybe she will never understand me, but I think now at least I understand her.

I was wobbly on my feet as I stood up and I nearly fell back down on the sand again. But then I felt a strong hand at my back, lifting me, and it was Baba, right there beside me.

"Baba?" I looked up at him. "Where is Bree? Is she OK?"

And then I saw her. Ali had her by the reins and was leading her back over to me. She had a small cut on her knee from crashing into the car.

"Is she lame?" Ali asked anxiously.

I shook my head. "The cut isn't deep. I don't think so."

Bree nudged me with her nose at that moment, as if to say, "I'm fine." All the same, I led her across the sand and trotted her to check the leg. She was sound.

"Leg me up?" I asked Baba.

"You're going to try again?" Baba looked worried and he hesitated at first, but I looked him straight in the eye and I said, "Tell fate that it will have to wait for another day."

It felt very strange, Mama, to be back up on Bree again. I was still shaking a little as I took up the reins. Luckily it took a while for everyone to leave the arena and for the jump to be rebuilt, so that gave me a chance to focus. Ali came over and he handed me the whip that I had dropped when I fell and then he looked up at me and said, "Try to go over it this time, instead of through it."

"Thanks for the advice," I smiled. I was about to turn Bree away when Baba clasped my hand and held it tight. "Haya." His voice was calm, full of confidence. "She can do it, Haya. Remember, keep your rhythm all the way to the fence, and then sit up and push her on for the last two strides."

And then they were gone and it was just me and Bree alone in the arena once more.

Bree didn't seem to be put off by the crash. She was pulling harder than ever on the reins as we circled in to take the upright and I had to check her firmly to say *No, I'm in charge*. She came back to me after that, settling into a bouncy canter to take the wide spread and then, as we rounded the corner, I saw the sunlight glinting off the car. It doesn't matter what Santi says,

you cannot pretend it isn't there. It was huge.

A million things rushed through my mind, Mama. But as I rode down to face the silver car, I felt the way I had on that very first day I rode Bree. I felt like my horse would take care of me. I felt safe. And at that moment I knew we could do it. "Come on, Bree," I whispered. "Go! Go now!"

I felt her strides quicken beneath me, her hocks strong and powerful working like pistons, and then she was gathering up. All I could sense was this awesome power as she took one perfect big bold stride to reach the fence and then she flew it. I mean really flew it – we must have cleared those top two rails of the spread with centimetres of air to spare. It was the most amazing feeling, as if we were suspended in the sky. Then I felt Bree grunt underneath me as she kicked out her hind legs to clear the last rail and we came down on the other side.

I could hear the applause, deafening as thunder, and I knew that the whole stadium had been holding their breath for us. The applause kept coming in waves and it carried us as we rode a lap, with me saluting to everyone, standing up in the stirrups with one hand on the reins, and Bree snorting and fretting at the bit, her tail held up and flowing behind her like a true Bedouin Arabian.

As we swooped round on our triumphant lap of the arena, I could see Baba and Ali. They were both clapping so hard and Frances was clapping along with them too and I smiled and waved back to them. Then a cheer rose up from the crowd and I looked up above Baba's head and I saw them raising my flag, blue and white, fluttering high on the fourth pole.

I was on such a high when we came back to the stables and everyone ran over to us. Zayn got to me first and he gave me a high five and then he realised that maybe this was the wrong thing to do, and he got flustered, and said, "Well done, Your Royal Highness."

I have never been more excited. We had jumped a car!

"She is the best horse in the world," I said to Zayn. And I meant it, Mama, she really is.

There was no time for celebration yet though. The vaulting was still to come and I had to get Bree ready. Zayn helped me to strip off her saddle, while I got the bucket and sponge and worked all over to cool her down. I used the sweat-scraper to get rid of the excess water and she looked so sleek, her coat shining a deep rich bay colour. I felt the smoothness of her and I thought about the bearskin rug. I'd had the chance to master my handstands on the wall with it. But I hadn't been able to practise since then on Bree. Well, I would get my chance soon enough.

Bashir's team went first in the vaulting. Their performance had a lot of yelling and whooping as they rode, but mostly it was the same old tricks.

Isn't it strange, Mama? They didn't want me to ride because I am a girl, but being a girl turned out to be a great advantage in the final event. Bashir and his men were big and heavy, cumbersome on their horses. Zayn and I, on the other hand, were small, nimble and light. We rode out into the arena with me doubling on the back of Yusef's grey and Zayn doubled on the back of Radi's chestnut – and proceeded to let our teammates toss us about like we were marionettes and they were playing our strings.

We vaulted off the horses and then bounced back up again as if the ground beneath us were a trampoline! At one point I stood up on the rump of Yusef's big grey at a canter and made a flying leap through the air to land neatly behind Attah on his bay mare. Meanwhile Zayn, riding on the back of Radi's chestnut, leapt from the other direction to land on the back of Yusef's grey in the spot I had left just moments before.

We rode backwards, waving to the crowds as we looked back over the horses' rumps, and then did flips to vault off, planting our feet on the ground as we struck the earth behind their thundering hooves. If the crowd had been cheering for Bashir's men before, now their applause was reverberating like thunder throughout the stadium, their feet stamping in time to the music. When I looked up at Baba in the Royal Box, there was such a smile on his face. It was as wide as the mouths of the lions at Al Nadwa palace.

The cheering was so loud in the arena that, when the time came for our finale, I could hardly hear Santi's words as he jogged Bree into the arena and handed her over to me.

"God protect you," Santi said. Then he legged me up and, as Yusef led the team up the centre line to take their last lap of the arena and wave their goodbyes to the crowds, I rode in and suddenly it was just the two of us in front of everyone, Bree and me.

She is such an amazing horse, Mama. I wish you could have met her. I wish you could see how much I love her.

"Let us show them the trick," I breathe to Bree. And I feel her gather herself beneath me and I urge her on so that her canter becomes a gallop. I look down and see the golden sand rushing away beneath her hooves. I know that if I fall this time then fate may take me. But I am not afraid.

I sit up straight on her back and let go of the reins. My hands stretch out to the sides like an aeroplane. I take another deep breath. I can feel the rhythm of her gallop, the pounding of her hooves, and my heart pounds too, *one-two-three*.

I am ready. I brace my hands against her silken coat and I pounce up so that I am like a cat on all fours. I hold myself there for just a moment, getting a grip on her withers, fingers spread wide, my weight in my hands and arms, legs ready to kick off. And then I push hard.

I think for a moment that I am going to go too far and topple forward on to her neck. But I keep my legs stiffened and my hands hold and the fingers do not slide this time, they stay planted firmly on Bree's withers. I straighten up, arch my back and stretch my toes to the sky, holding the pose with all of my strength.

And I know that, no matter what happens, I will not fall.

Epilogue

Princess Haya Bint Al Hussein was twelve years old when she led the Jordanian Royal Stables team to victory against the Mounted Police in the King's Cup. It was the first time that Al Hummar had taken the coveted prize in over a decade.

At age thirteen, Princess Haya was the first female rider to represent Jordan internationally in equestrian sport, winning an Individual Bronze Medal in showjumping at the Pan-Arab Equestrian Games in 1992. She remains the sole female competitor ever to win a medal in Pan-Arab equestrian sport.

Controversy surrounded Princess Haya's decision to become a professional showjumper, but her father always supported her unconditionally. When she became the only woman in Jordan to hold a heavy

vehicle licence so that she could drive her horses to compete on the European circuit, the King nicknamed her 'The Trucker'. He loved to hear about her decidedly un-royal experiences and stories of life on the road.

In 2000, Princess Haya was chosen for the Olympic showjumping team to compete in Sydney and carried the Jordanian flag in the opening ceremony, taking her rightful place among the best athletes in the world. Tragically, King Hussein died just prior to the games.

Two years later, riding at the World Equestrian Games at Jerez de la Frontera in Spain, Princess Haya met her future husband, Sheik Mohammed Bin Rashid

Al-Maktoum, ruler of Dubai. They married in 2004 and have two children, Her Highness Sheikha Al-Jalila and His Highness Sheikh Zayed.

Today Princess Haya holds one of the highest honours in the equestrian world as the elected head of the International Equestrian Federation – the FEI. Her tenure has revolutionised the role of the presidency and she was voted into an unprecedented second term in 2010.

Princess Haya's brother, Prince Ali, whom she once stuck in a dumb waiter, is the Vice-president of the world football association, FIFA, representing Asia.

In memory of her mother, Her Majesty the late Queen Alia, Princess Haya founded Tkiyet Um Ali in 2003, the first food-aid NGO in the Arab world, and became the Chair of its Board of Directors. She was also the first Arab and first woman to serve as World Food Programme Goodwill Ambassador and has been appointed by the UN as a Messenger of Peace.

Bint Al-Reeh, the orphaned foal who was raised by the Princess, went on to win many jumping competitions, before living out her days in well-earned retirement at Al Hummar stables.